Burke and the Lines of Torres Vedras

Tom Williams

ISBN: 978-1-8383975-7-9
First published by Big Red 2023

Contents

JAMES FLORENCE BURKE

Born Ireland 1771

Enlisted Regiment of Dillon (France). Saw active service in Sainte Domingue. Surrendered to British in 1793

Detached for special duties at the War Office

1793/4: confidential duties in Ireland

1798: confidential duties in Egypt

1805: confidential duties in Argentina

1806: attached to British forces in Buenos Aires

1806: promoted to Captain

1807: confidential mission to the Spanish court

1808: promoted to Major

1808: diplomatic posting to Brazil

1809: diplomatic posting to Argentina

1809: attached to General Hill in Spain

1809: confidential work in France

1810: attached to General Beresford's staff in Lisbon

1815: confidential work with Allied occupation forces in Paris

1815: attached to the Hussars of Croy. Saw action at Waterloo

For those who like to keep track of these things, the action in this book takes place in 1810 and follows directly on from the end of *Burke and the Pimpernel Affair*. There are some references to his earlier adventures but you can enjoy this book even if you haven't read any of the others.

CHAPTER 1: An interview with Colonel Gordon

Burke kicked his horse into a canter. It wasn't really the done thing: Rotten Row was a place to see and be seen. A gentle trot might be acceptable but anything more than that was frowned on. James Burke, though, wanted to prove to himself, and anyone who asked, that his leg was truly healed and a turn along Hyde Park on a borrowed cavalry charger seemed the easiest way to do that. He could, he supposed, have ridden out on the turnpike towards Bath, but the packed earth of the road was not kind to a horse's legs and the turnpike fee, though affordable, was an unnecessary expense. The Row was convenient and free and, even at a canter, there was the chance of meeting an old friend – or making a new one. He could rein in quickly enough at the sight of a pretty face.

He slowed as he approached the end of Hyde Park. Kensington Gardens stretched before him but the ditch of a ha-ha separated the palace gardens from the public park and Rotten Row ended abruptly at the boundary.

He could remember when he first came to London and Kensington was a little village well away from town. Since then, London had grown and there was just the Park between Kensington and the edge of the metropolis. Riding there hardly worked his horse up to a sweat. The growth of the city had left surprisingly few decent places to ride out that were easily reached from his quarters at the Tower.

He turned his horse and set off back at a gentle trot, slowing to salute any carriages that carried a coat of arms on the doors. He recognised none of these people, but it never hurt to be polite. You could never know when you might need influential friends.

James Burke had all too often come across officers whose careers were built on the influence of friends who could have a word in the right ears at the War Office or help out with the money needed to buy a more senior commission. These were not options open to the son of an Irish Catholic whose income depended on the pittance he received from a handful of farms where potatoes struggled to grow in the boggy soil. So while younger, less able, men won glory and honour on the field of battle, he was still skulking about as a confidential agent of His Majesty or, as everyone else called it, as a spy. And since he was wounded springing prisoners from a castle in the heart of Paris, he was not even allowed to conduct his usual trade any more. Colonel Gordon, his chief in the Army's nascent intelligence service, insisted that he could not go back into the field until an Army surgeon had attested that his leg was fully recovered.

He stretched it now, rising in the saddle. Of course it was recovered. The wound had been tended by the physician who served the Empress Josephine, though this was, obviously, not a detail that was shared with his English doctor. The Army surgeon knew only that the work had been done by a Frenchman and, as far as he was concerned, no French doctor could be trusted to do a decent job. So the doctor vacillated and Gordon allowed Burke no missions that might tax his strength. He had even found himself loaned out to the despised Alien Office. Posing as a French émigré, his mission was to get close to another Frenchman who was ostensibly escaping persecution but who was suspected of being a spy for Napoleon. The man was foolish enough to trust Burke and was now rotting in an English gaol. Burke knew he had done a good job, but he felt no satisfaction in it, and he was pleased when the Alien Office had finished with his services.

At least working in London meant that he had been able to spend Christmas with William Brown and the estimable Molly Brown at the Crown – the tavern she ran near the Tower. If his fellow officers had known that he spent Christmas with his sergeant, they would undoubtedly have disapproved. But the relationship between Burke and William was hardly typical of that between officer and man. On their undercover missions, the two relied implicitly on each other and they had the closeness of men who had held each other's lives in their hands on more than one occasion.

After Christmas, he was finally pronounced fit enough to be sent on short missions in Europe, though not to France. His exploits there had, Gordon ruled, made it unwise to send him back for a while. "Word has it," he said, "that their secret police have a particular interest in meeting you again." Burke thought of the way he and William had freed prisoners from under the nose of Napoleon's police chief, Fouché, and could well believe that the French would dearly like to find him back in their country.

So the weeks passed and Burke wondered if Gordon had decided he was no longer suited for more serious work. Finally, in April, he was called to the colonel's office in Horse Guards.

* * *

"I'm glad to see you well recovered, Burke."

"I'm feeling fighting fit, sir."

Gordon looked at him appraisingly. "Yes, I think you are." He rose from his chair and picked up a bottle from a table in the corner of the room. "Sherry?"

The old man was in an unusually mellow mood, Burke thought. "Don't mind if I do, sir."

Gordon allowed him time for a sip before starting to speak.

"You're good at all this dirty work." An expression of distaste passed across Burke's face and Gordon grinned. "How would you like to see things from the other side?" Then, when Burke looked puzzled, he added, "Poacher turned gamekeeper."

"Sir?"

"There's a problem with our friends in Lisbon." He sipped his sherry. "Some of them aren't our friends."

"The Portuguese have been very loyal, sir. Notably more so than the Spanish."

Gordon flapped a hand dismissively. "Just so, Burke. Salt of the earth and all that. I'm not talking about the common soldiers, or most of the generals. But it seems that there are doubts about the loyalty of some senior chaps. Not to put too fine a point on it, they are believed to be in contact with the French. We can't prove anything, of course. We can't even be absolutely certain that anything is amiss. But I'd like us to have my own man out there so I know what's really going on. A man who understands the dark arts of espionage. A man rather like you. You've shown your mettle with that job you did for the Alien Office a few weeks back. How do you feel about doing the same sort of thing out in Portugal?"

It wasn't really a question.

"It sounds a fascinating opportunity, sir."

"Jolly good. I thought you'd like it. You're always trying to get back into uniform, aren't you?" That wasn't a question either. "Well now you can. We're going to give you some sort of liaison post. Lisbon is filled with officers liaising on this or liaising on that. One more will hardly be noticed. Once you're there, you keep your eyes peeled and let us know if there's anything doesn't look right."

Gordon looked out of the window. It was already turning dark and the clouds threatened rain.

"Probably not the best of times to be crossing the Channel. Spend another week or so in London, why don't you? Let that man of yours have a bit of time with his wife."

Burke was surprised that Gordon remembered William had a wife, let alone that he wanted Sgt Brown to have more time to enjoy domestic bliss. This sudden caring side to Gordon made him nervous.

"I'm sure we'll both be grateful, sir."

"I'm sure he deserves some leave." Burke realised that the idea of leave seemed to embrace only his sergeant. "It will give you time to come to terms with the political situation in Lisbon. I'm sending one of those Foreign Office chappies to see you. He'll explain it all."

He threw back the last of his sherry. "Any questions?" He didn't wait for an answer. "Good luck!"

Burke hadn't even finished his drink. Too late now. "Thank you, sir." He tried to think of something to add, but Gordon had already turned his attention to the paperwork on his desk. Burke saluted. Gordon wouldn't even notice but he felt he had to do something to conclude the interview. Then he walked out and set off back to the Tower.

* * *

The 'chappie' from the Foreign Office was called Thoms and he arrived at the Tower the next day armed with an alarming bundle of paperwork.

Burke raised a sceptical eyebrow, "Is this really necessary? I'm looking for a spy, not trying to run the government."

Thoms, an earnest young man with spectacles, jerked his head nervously up and down, like one of the puppets about to suffer a beating at the hands of Mr Punch.

"I'm afraid you are going to run the country in a manner of speaking."

"Really?" Burke's tone was chilly.

"You are officially to be a liaison officer to the Portuguese Army."

"I know that. I carry the odd message to and fro but I spend most of my time staying out of the way and listening at doors and windows until I have a better idea of what's going on. I'm hardly concerning myself with political matters."

"Perhaps I could talk you through the key points before you plunge into the detail."

Burke, who had no intention of plunging into the detail, agreed that this might be a good idea.

"You are aware that Portugal is a monarchy, sir?"

"Don't condescend to me, Thoms. I'm not only aware of it, but I've spent time in their wretched court."

Thoms, who had fallen naturally into the role of an expert tutor faced with a bright, but ignorant, student, looked confused.

"But the court is ..."

"In Brazil, Thoms. I know. I was there."

"Oh!" There was a pause and Burke could see Thoms steeling himself to ask a question. *Oh, please, please don't*, he thought but here it came. Everyone who knew anything about the court in Rio de Janeiro asked the same question once they knew he'd been there. "Did you ever meet ..."

"Princess Carlota? Yes, I did. I've probably still got the scratch marks on my back."

Thoms blushed. Burke felt that he may have had too sheltered an upbringing to progress to any really interesting postings in the Foreign Office.

"Is it true that she..." James cast an especially evil glance at the young man who suddenly developed a powerful interest in his papers. "Anyway, with the court in Rio, Portugal is now technically a colony of Brazil."

Burke laughed. He knew he shouldn't have but everything about his time with the frankly deranged Princess Carlota and her mad make-believe court cut off on the wrong side of the world had been insane. The idea that the Prince Regent had decided that Portugal was a mere colony of the pleasure palace he had built on a bay in South America was too ridiculous to take seriously. Yet here was Mr Thoms apparently taking it very seriously indeed.

"So who's actually running the country? Even that bunch of lunatics can't believe they can rule from that far away."

"There's a Council of Regency."

"Who are they?"

"Basically people who weren't important enough to be included among the thousand or so courtiers who were evacuated from Lisbon."

"So is there anybody in Portugal who knows what they are doing?"

"Well, yes. Portugal is now a country dedicated to total war. The army, in practice, runs everything."

Burke began to see where this was going.

"Who runs the army?"

"We do. Well, strictly speaking it's General Beresford."

"God help us!"

"You are familiar with General Beresford, sir?"

"You could say so. He was the bloody idiot who lost Buenos Aires for us in 1806. I was there. It is fair to say we did not get along."

"Then you might understand why Colonel Gordon is so enthusiastic that you master the politics of the situation, sir."

Burke understood well enough. He had been in Buenos Aires, ensuring that there was no serious resistance to the British invasion. It had been a triumph. The British had come to liberate a Spanish province that was already simmering on the edge of revolt. And then Beresford's total lack of any sensitivity to local political realities meant that he cheerfully antagonised the population to the point where the people had risen to force the British out. The Spanish might be evil colonialist exploiters, but at least they spoke the language and understood what compromises had to be made.

"How much damage has Beresford done?"

Burke could see that Thoms was uncomfortable with the directness of the question but, after a brief pause, he did his best to give an honest answer.

"We don't know, sir. He's a good enough general and he's doing a splendid job with reorganising the army and integrating command with our forces, but we have the impression that he is rather annoying a lot of people."

"'You have the impression.' Don't we have diplomats and suchlike to keep us abreast of these things?"

"We do, yes. Indeed we have a Mr Charles Stuart, who is the British Minister to Lisbon. But, in the current situation, he can do nothing without Beresford and all diplomatic messages pass through the general's office. You can see why we are not quite as *au fait* with the situation as we might wish."

"And might that have anything to do with the reason that I am going to be there playing at being a diplomat?"

"Colonel Gordon thought it might be helpful. Two birds with one stone, so to speak. One of our main concerns is that Beresford might have annoyed some senior officials enough to make them prefer French rule to his." Remembering the fiasco at Buenos Aires, Burke feared this might well be the case.

"Is it possible that the people that General Beresford is annoying might include the Council of Regency?"

"Almost certainly, sir."

"And he's driving them to the French?"

"Oh no, sir. They were betraying their country to the French already."

* * *

Burke's meeting with Mr Thoms was taking place in a quiet office that the Tower Adjutant thought was ideally suited to put the man from the Foreign Office at ease without allowing himself to have delusions of being anybody important. This meant a couple of comfortable armchairs, a desk, and a table, but only a small window and that looking out onto the back of the Tower's walls rather than the famous White Tower. It did, though, run to a small, locked cupboard to which

Burke had been given the key. Now he unlocked it and drew out a large decanter of whisky and two glasses.

"I think you need to explain," he said. And Mr Thoms explained.

The Council of Regency had been set up to balance different centres of power against each other. For example, it had representatives from the north of the country (which generated most of Portugal's money) and the south (where the capital and political power lay). During the French occupation of Portugal, members of the Council of Regency had often been more concerned with trying to seize power within the Council than with defeating the French. In fact, some had actively collaborated with their occupiers.

The obvious thing was to appoint a new council but Beresford had at least learned something from his experience in Buenos Aires. The Portuguese were our brave allies and nothing was to be done that suggested that Britain was in any way trying to take control of the country. So the British stood aside as the Portuguese fought and politicked over the formation of the new body. The government in London had appointed a British Minister who should sit on the Council and represent British interests but, though increasingly unsubtle hints were being dropped, nobody dared insist on his being added to the Council membership. The Portuguese knew they would have to appoint him eventually, but they relished the opportunity they had to demonstrate their independence and intended to make him wait as long as possible, just to prove they could. And without any outsiders to hold the ring, the squabbling over who was to sit on the Council seemed set to last for years.

"Meanwhile, the government is in chaos. The French have left much of the country in ruins; there's barely enough grain to feed their own population, let alone all the British troops in the place; everyone's looking sideways at the men who got too cosy with the French and wondering whether to denounce them; and there are still cabals plotting to move power to Porto or bring back the Regent from Brazil. It's an atmosphere where treachery and betrayal inevitably thrive. I wish you luck of it."

Burke was, by nature, an optimist, but now he sat quietly drinking his whisky. It seemed that he would have his work cut out for him in Lisbon.

Thoms watched him for a while and then, as the silence was stretched to the point where it became awkward, he cleared his throat and put his papers on the table.

"I'll leave these with you," he said. "It's our assessments of the main runners and riders in Lisbon. Should be useful. You'll need to mug it up here and leave the notes when you travel. We can't have the Portuguese read what we really think of them."

Burke glanced at the pile of paperwork and grunted.

"I'll be off."

Thoms closed the door quietly behind him, while Burke poured himself another drink.

CHAPTER 2: General Beresford

General William Carr Beresford wiped his brow with a handkerchief. He had quite a lot of brow to wipe. He had a naturally high forehead and had started to lose what hair he was born with when he was still in his thirties. By now he looked considerably older than his forty-one years.

He felt damnably hot. That was the trouble with Lisbon in February: cold enough to need a fire in the grate but then the weather could grow unaccountably hotter. With the fire still burning, he would order the windows flung wide. He would be sweating even as the breeze through the windows made the room irritatingly chilly. Sometimes he thought the weather was conspiring against him. Why not? Conspiring against the British seemed to be the national sport.

He missed campaigning: yes, it was uncomfortable; yes, there was never quite enough to eat; yes, days spent in the saddle left him wincing whenever he sat on a hard chair, but he longed to breathe fresh air again and be away from the wretched Portuguese and their interminable arguments about money. They were costing Britain a fortune and still they complained. It was as if they felt they were doing the British a favour by allowing their ally to drive the French out of the country for them.

And now, as if it wasn't enough to be constantly harassed by the Portuguese, he was being pushed about by Wellington as well.

He picked up the letter that lay on the desk before him and read it once more.

To Marshal Beresford
Viseu. 19th April 1810

Col. Gordon is anxious to place one of his men in Lisbon to ensure the security of my plans for defensive action in Portugal. It would be of immeasurable assistance were he to be nominally attached to your staff with a responsibility for liaison between the British and Portuguese armies. In such a role he should be well placed to report the exact state of affairs regarding any continuing disaffection among elements of the Portuguese army which might encourage them to favour the French interest.

Gordon's man is Major Burke, but I have arranged for him to be breveted colonel in the hope of flattering the Portuguese that we will not inflict a simple major on them.

Whilst he will maintain the fiction that his responsibilities are to yourself, he will largely act independently and will report solely to Col. Gordon. I would be grateful if you could ensure that Burke is furnished with a secure means of communication between Lisbon and London.

Col Burke will be paid from Col Gordon's funds, but I would be very much obliged to you if you would send me a nominal list of the other British officers serving with the Portuguese army or in a liaison position, specifying the regiments to which they belong and their periods of service detached from their proper regiments.

I have the honour to be, &c &c

There was nothing to like about the letter and several things that were downright insulting. Make a man a viscount and he thought he was better than his colleagues! Wellesley (he couldn't get used to calling him Wellington) was inflicting one of Gordon's creatures on him. They were simply spies, slinking about looking for tittle-tattle to relay back to their masters in London. And he, Marshal of the Portuguese army, was to provide "a secure means of communication" so that the awful little creature could tell his tales behind the backs of better men.

Something about this spy was pulling at some vague thread of memory. James Burke: the name rang a bell.

Then he remembered. Buenos Aires and some arrogant young officer – a lowly captain then, he thought – telling him how he should be running his administration. Beresford had sent him on his way with a flea in his ear.

Wasn't there some story about him treating with the rebels? Hadn't there been some sort of enquiry? Whatever the story, the damn fellow had no business turning up here with his ideas about how to treat the natives you've liberated from occupation.

He'd have to keep an eye on this Burke fellow. And God help him if he stepped out of line this time.

CHAPTER 3: Welcome to Lisbon

Once again Burke found himself sailing for Lisbon on the *Statira*. Captain Boys was still in command and welcomed him aboard with apparently genuine pleasure.

"Colonel now, is it? Congratulations, sir. It seems your last campaign must have been good to you. Were you at Talavera, sir?"

"I regret that I was not, sir, although my sergeant had that honour."

Captain Boys at once suggested that Brown be summoned from his berth amidships to dine with Burke and the ship's officers. "If that's acceptable to you, colonel. We stand less on ceremony at sea than you may be used to and we have heard so much of that battle. I know we would welcome the opportunity to dine with someone who was there."

James was happy to agree, though he knew William would find it difficult to talk about Talavera. His sergeant would be sure to describe a great victory. A victory had been desperately needed and Captain Boys and his crew wanted news of the glorious triumph there. Thousands of lives had been thrown away to give the country that triumph and William understood its importance better than most – even if the horror of it still haunted him.

It was a pleasant enough voyage. William told his story of Talavera well and when Burke let slip that Brown had fought with Nelson at the Nile, he was a hero of the wardroom and dined with the officers every night.

Their arrival in Lisbon was all that Burke could have wished for too. A captain and two privates were waiting for him to disembark. The officer saluted smartly as he stepped onto Portuguese soil and his men hurried forward to load Burke's baggage onto a mule cart that waited on the quayside.

"You've been billeted with a Snr Lopez. He's a merchant and he's doing great business supplying the British, so he's always happy to put up our officers. The fact that we pay him a fortune for the privilege helps too. He keeps a good table. You'll like him."

"And my man?"

"We thought he could mess with the port garrison."

"I think not." Burke had seen enough colonels exercising the petty prerogatives of power to know the tone to take. "He's my personal servant and I require him readily to hand. I'm sure Snr Lopez has staff. You can find him a place with them."

William stood by, doing his best to look like the humble officer's servant he so often pretended to be. In truth, he doubted that it was really necessary to sleep under the same roof as Burke, but it sounded like a comfortable billet with excellent food, so he appreciated the effort being made on his behalf.

The captain looked momentarily taken aback by the request but recovered himself quickly.

"I'm sure we can sort something out, sir."

Burke smiled. He could get used to being a colonel.

* * *

Burke settled into his new quarters easily enough. William had been found a room with the other servants, tucked away in the garret, and he reported that it was clean and the bed was comfortable, which, he claimed, was all he cared about. Burke had noticed that there were a couple of maids who were young and pretty and he imagined that William cared about that too, but was maintaining a tactful silence on the subject.

Snr Lopez was a widower living alone, which was probably for the best. Burke's record with other men's wives and daughters meant that a bachelor household was likely to make his stay less complicated.

He left William unpacking his travelling trunk: Brown's official role was as a servant after all.

Burke did not expect to enjoy his next visit at much as he had enjoyed his brief but agreeable meeting with Snr Lopez. An appointment with Marshal Beresford was not something to look forward to. Unfortunately, military etiquette meant it was impossible to avoid. While Gordon had made it very clear that he was to work independently of Beresford, his cover on Beresford's staff meant a meeting was inevitable. Even if he had somehow managed to duck out of the obligation, a failure to meet his nominal commander at all would hardly have supported his cover story. He could only hope that the meeting would be brief and that, with luck, Beresford would not remember that they had met before.

It was a futile hope, of course.

The first indication that things were not going to go smoothly was when he was kept waiting to see the Marshal. Colonels were generally not left to cool their heels in an outer office under the eyes of a clerk who was clearly uncomfortable with the situation.

There was a carriage clock on the mantel piece and Burke noticed that he waited exactly nine minutes. That was, he thought, nicely judged. Keeping him waiting more than ten minutes would be unmistakably insulting and could lead to comment among his staff, potentially embarrassing Beresford at least as much as Burke. Nine minutes was long enough to irritate but was not (quite) downright rude.

After the nine minutes a captain emerged from behind a pair of tall doors – Burke suspected mahogany but could not be sure – and summoned him in.

Beresford was sat behind his desk, making a great show of signing some papers. Burke stood to attention – unusual for a colonel calling on his commanding officer, but it seemed safest.

Eventually Beresford finished signing and sprinkled sand on the documents to blot them. Only then did he deign to acknowledge Burke's presence. He gestured vaguely towards a chair and Burke sat.

"Colonel Burke, we meet again."

So much for him having forgotten Buenos Aires.

"Delighted to make your acquaintance again, sir."

Beresford sniffed. "I have been told that you are nominally on my staff but you are not to make yourself useful to me."

Another sniff.

Burke wondered if he could get away without replying. It wasn't, after all, as if he had been asked a question.

There was a long silence. It seemed he couldn't get away without replying after all.

"I hope that my activities will be useful to the Army generally and thus of benefit to you."

The sweat was standing out on the Marshal's forehead. Burke tried not to look at it.

"You report directly to Gordon, Burke. You are here to spy on me and I am told that I must make provision for your messages to be sent directly to Horse Guards. Not using diplomatic channels, because heaven forfend that I might be able to read whatever tittle tattle you might be passing on behind the backs of your superiors."

The simplest thing, thought Burke, might be to explain to Beresford exactly why he was there. But if Gordon had intended Beresford to know his mission, wouldn't he have told him? Perhaps it was best to leave the Marshal guessing.

Burke said nothing immediately while he considered the best approach to take.

Beresford drew a handkerchief from his sleeve and pressed it to his face, mopping at the sweat dripping down that great forehead.

Burke watched and realised just how much he hated the man. Beresford had thrown away victory in Buenos Aires – a victory that Burke had been instrumental in delivering – and good men had died because of his stupidity. If Burke's instructions meant Beresford's life would be that little bit less comfortable, he would take great pleasure in following those instructions to the letter.

"I'm afraid my orders do not allow me to share details of my mission, even with such an esteemed officer as yourself." There was a pulse, Burke noticed, in a vein below Beresford's eye. He wondered if there was any chance of the man succumbing to an apoplectic fit but, regrettably, this seemed unlikely. "There have been concerns about the loyalty of some of the Portuguese generals."

Beresford spluttered with indignation. Perhaps there was some chance of an apoplectic fit after all.

"How dare you sir! How dare you imply that any of the brave gentlemen I have the honour to command might not be entirely committed to the war against France."

Burke gave the most insincere smile he could muster. "Perhaps I have misunderstood, sir. I know that several members of the Council of Regency have lost their posts because of uncertainty about their loyalty. Perhaps the problem is confined to the political gentlemen and the army remains untainted by treason." He put his hand to his forehead as if he had been struck with an idea.

"You were concerned that I might be of no use to you, sir. Perhaps that is the answer. Perhaps you could have me attend some of the meetings that must take place between your officers and the Portuguese. I can take the load off some of your staff and, if you would like me to, I could report my opinion of the Portuguese. You would even be in possession of my conclusions before I had reported to Colonel Gordon."

Burke wondered if there was the slightest possibility that Beresford ever played cards with his officers. Every thought that passed through Beresford's mind was unmistakably signalled on his face. Anyone facing him across the gaming table would leave a great deal richer than he arrived.

First there was fury at being reminded that some of those he worked alongside might not be of unimpeachable loyalty. Then came the idea that he could pass responsibility for these concerns onto Burke. There was a narrowing of the eyes as he contemplated ways in which, once in a position to order Burke around, he might be able to teach his insolent subordinate a lesson – and have Burke running his errands for him at the same time.

It was the possibility of putting one over on Gordon that convinced him, though. Burke thought the man might actually salivate at the prospect of having Gordon's agent reporting to him. It didn't seem to have occurred to Beresford that Burke might simply have been lying and had no intention of revealing his conclusions before laying them before the spy master at Horse Guards.

Beresford nodded sagely, attempting, Burke thought, to assume the mien of a political giant, moving his creatures to control Portugal from his position as the British Government's chief military representative. The terrifying thing, Burke realised, was that he was more or less correct. With the court in Brazil, the Council of Regency in disarray, and no other government to run the country, Beresford had somehow become the *de facto* leader of Portugal. Burke could almost sympathise with those Portuguese who would rather throw in their lot with the French.

"Let me think about it," said Beresford, as if he had to ponder weighty affairs of state. Burke was not fooled. He had taken the bait, but wanted to keep Burke waiting to learn his fate. Burke carefully composed his face to look appropriately grateful that his case was even being considered and, with a half bow, he left to set off back to Snr Lopez's house and the fine dinner that had been promised him.

* * *

The next morning Burke rose late and took his time over a breakfast of bread and ham. He lingered as long as he could over coffee, but it looked as though Beresford was not going to respond that morning.

Rather than a sit around wasting time, he decided to take a walk around Lisbon. He was a soldier after all. It was always a good idea to reconnoitre the field before battle commenced.

Snr Lopez's house was only a short walk from the docks, but the street where he lived had nothing in common with the roads that Burke expected to find in most dock areas. The straight streets lined with elegant houses had an unmistakably Spanish feel. It rather reminded him of Madrid or Buenos Aires, except that all the buildings seemed to be new. Then he remembered that much of Lisbon had been destroyed by an earthquake in 1755: the streets he was exploring had all been built in the last 50 years or so.

He followed the road, which ran gently downhill until it opened into what seemed to be the main square of the city. Three sides were made up of grand buildings, with the fourth opening directly onto the River Tagus. Lisbon's prosperity depended on its port, so having the architectural centre of the city right down by the water made sense.

In the centre of the plaza a statue of a man on horseback stared out over the river. He seemed quite a lonely figure. The square, which in normal times, Burke thought, should be thronged with people, was almost deserted. A few market stalls were huddled together in one corner, somehow making the great paved space seem even emptier than if they had not been there. Napoleon's blockade on trade with England and her allies was clearly having some effect and the wharves along the river, which should have been crowded with ships bringing goods to sell in the plaza, were almost deserted. Just one Portuguese merchantman was being unloaded, its flag hanging limply at its mast. The Portuguese flag was white, with the coat of arms of the Kingdom in the middle but, with no wind blowing, all Burke could see was a white flag, which seemed an unfortunate omen at a time of war. The smell of coffee as they unloaded, though, was reassuring evidence that ships were still making the long voyage across the Atlantic from Brazil.

Burke walked across to the statue. His footsteps seeming to echo unnaturally loudly. He looked up at the mounted figure. An inscription told him that this was King José I who, according to the plaque, had died only thirty or so years ago but, alone in all that space, Burke felt like an explorer looking at the tomb of some ancient king lost in a vast desert. He could hardly believe that only 50 years ago the leaders of Portugal were able to think on this sort of scale. That, he supposed, was what war and invasion and the collapse of government would do to you.

At the far end of the wharves, as if trying to distance themselves as much as possible from the Portuguese vessel, were four ships carrying Union flags, presumably the latest convoy to bring grain to feed Wellington's army. It was astonishing how much wheat the army went through and, with Portugal struggling to feed its own population, almost every bushel was carried from England. Further out to sea, Burke could see the frigate that had escorted them.

Half a dozen carts were drawn up, ready to carry the grain to the Army's warehouses, but there was no sign of them being loaded. Burke, with nothing else to do, drifted over to see what the delay was.

A red-coated lieutenant, presumably in charge, was gesticulating angrily toward one of the carts, while the Portuguese driver shrugged. Closer to, Burke could see the cart crooked on what was clearly a broken axle. Looking at the others he saw another that was tilted to one side – a clear indication of another axle about to go.

He wondered if the sea air rotted the wood of the carts or if Portuguese carriage-makers were incompetent. Then again, knowing the Army, somebody had decided to save time by overloading the carts and cutting down on the number of journeys they would have to make before all the cargo was carried to the stores. There was always a captain somewhere with bright ideas about how to save time and there was always a lieutenant to take the blame when they went wrong. The lieutenant who was going to take the blame today was swearing fluently in English and, slightly less fluently, in Portuguese but nothing he said was going to help.

There was nothing to be done until somebody had arrived with a replacement axle, so Burke turned away and continued his walk along the Tagus.

Almost immediately, he reached the end of the elegant modern streets. With the river to his right, the ground on the left rose steeply and the houses were a jumble of older buildings on twisting lanes that ran up to the castle at the top of the hill. The rock seemed to have protected buildings here from the worst of the earthquake. Some fishing boats were unloading their catches, giving the area a distinctive smell that Burke imagined would not be welcome in the grand square he had just left.

He followed a man carrying a crate of fish up through the alleyways. The fellow stopped here and there, selling to eating houses that could serve meals to maybe half a dozen customers at a time. As Burke followed him up he passed bars, and a few shops selling vegetables and one with a window full of pottery mugs and plates. The patterns on the crockery were bright but crude and he suspected that they had been made locally. The place was obviously not rich, but it was lively and the people, in decent clothes, if occasionally bare-footed, seemed at least as prosperous as the working poor of London.

At the top of the hill was the castle that dominated Lisbon. He abandoned following the fish merchant to take a good look at the place.

It was obviously old – he vaguely remembered someone saying it dated back to the time of the Moorish occupation – but it had been extended and rebuilt over the years and the walls were in good condition. It didn't look as if it would be particularly useful in the war against France though. It was definitely a strong point, but a garrison in the castle would be trapped there, unable to sally out and clear an enemy from the alleys of the town below: a maze of steep, narrow streets that provided ideal conditions for attackers to trap any force venturing out of the fortress. And, in any case, Lisbon stood isolated in the south of the country. The French could ignore it. If they took the rest of the peninsula they had only to wait and eventually Lisbon would have to surrender. It was a useful port to supply the British armies from, but it seemed peripheral to the wider war that Wellington was fighting. Beresford, he thought, was welcome to the place.

It was less than twenty-four hours after he had taken his walk around the castle that he was to realise how wrong he was.

CHAPTER 4: Colonel Fletcher

When a messenger arrived at his lodgings the next morning, he assumed it was a summons from Beresford but it was from a Colonel Richard Fletcher.

"Who the hell is Richard Fletcher?" he asked Brown.

William, usually a reliable source of information on practically every officer in the British Army, looked nonplussed.

"Can't really say, sir. He was at Talavera, I know that. Some sort of engineer. He was on Wellington's staff: I've heard Nosey thinks well of him."

Burke grunted noncommittally. Engineers, as far as he was concerned, were hardly real soldiers at all, though he knew they had their uses. On the other hand, Burke, like almost every other officer in the Army, had come to have a high opinion of Wellington and if the commander rated this Fletcher fellow, he supposed the man must have something to recommend him. In any case, it could do no harm to call on him.

It took him a while to find Colonel Fletcher's office. He wasn't near Beresford's headquarters or among the cluster of offices that formed a sort of British military colony in the shadow of the castle. It seemed that Fletcher preferred the new town where he had commandeered an elegant mansion in the middle of one of the blocks of houses, so new that some still had masons working on the decorations over the doorways.

Burke could see the advantages of such a billet. It was modern, airy and did not smell of fish. On the other hand, it was inconveniently situated. The castle loomed over it, but there were no roads on this side. Fletcher's working day must start with an inconveniently long journey through the narrow streets that Burke had explored the day before and, if he spent his evenings dining with his fellow officers, he faced an equally long journey back in the dark.

Burke's first conclusion was that Fletcher must be a solitary creature. He shared the prejudice of many soldiers and believed that Engineers were overly fond of surveying equipment and diagrams of bridges and preferred an evening with their charts and tables to the company of fellow officers and the ladies of the town.

As he approached the house, though, the door opened and two young men emerged in smart red coats and white breeches with cross belts that carried badges that caught the sun. They were too far away for him to be certain but the badges, he thought, were those of the Corps of Royal Engineers. Certainly the uniform could well be that of the Engineers though, like most corps, they lacked the facings that would firmly identify their unit. Was Fletcher entertaining his junior officers at his home? The fellow was, perhaps, more interesting than Burke had been expecting.

As he arrived at the door, another officer clattered up on horseback. The door opened before the man could dismount and a servant hurried out to take the bridle as the officer swung himself to the ground and hurried past Burke into the building. Curiouser and curiouser, thought Burke. The servant holding the horse was in civilian dress, but carried himself with the bearing of a soldier. What exactly was going on at Fletcher's residence?

As the officer had left the door open, Burke simply followed him in. Judging from the comings and goings, Fletcher seemed to run a relaxed establishment and Burke rather fancied the idea of a look at what was going on before any formal interview.

He barely had time to take in the beautifully proportioned entrance hall and the landscape paintings decorating the walls before an angry shout drew his attention to two more servants apparently there to greet visitors. Again, they had the air of military men – an impression made even stronger by the way that they were pointing pistols dead centre at his chest.

A door opened and yet another officer stepped into the hall. Was Fletcher having a party or was he providing some sort of transit camp for Engineers?

"Who the hell are you?" The fellow spoke, it seemed to Burke with the arrogance of youth and a notable disregard for Burke's new rank.

"I'm Colonel James Burke. Shouldn't you be saluting?"

"I don't care what rank you carry. You have no business in here."

"On the contrary, Colonel Fletcher invited me to call on him."

"It's normal to knock and have yourself announced."

"The door was open. People were coming and going. It seemed natural to come in."

One of the men pointing a pistol at Burke spoke up. "I keep saying that a guard on the door would be a good idea."

"Keeping the door closed would be a good idea, Jenkins. What the hell happened?"

"Captain Jakes, sir. Just rushed in. Carson is outside holding his horse. Door was only open for a moment, sir."

The officer turned to call into the room he had emerged from. "Orderly!"

Another man in civilian dress appeared.

"Find the colonel and ask if he is expecting a Colonel Burke. If he is, escort him to Fletcher's office." The orderly hurried off up the stairs that curved elegantly around the hallway. The officer gestured at the guards. "If he stirs a muscle, shoot him." Then, without any further comment, he vanished back into the room he had come out of.

There was a clatter of feet on the stairs as the orderly returned. "Colonel Fletcher says he's expected." The guards lowered their pistols with, it seemed to Burke, some reluctance. He began to think that they might well really have shot him.

"Follow me," said the orderly and, after a significant pause, "sir."

The stairs led to a corridor with doors on either side. Burke could hear the murmuring of many voices and had the impression of being in a building full of busy people, but there was nobody to be seen.

He followed the orderly to a door at the end of the corridor, which he realised must lead into a room at the front of the house overlooking the street. The orderly knocked and Burke waited for the usual invitation to enter. Instead the door opened and a man in his early forties, but with the energy of somebody much younger, appeared with his arm outstretched to take Burke's hand, which he preceded to pump vigorously up and down.

"Sorry about the confusion. Not your fault. Knew you were a spy. Shouldn't have expected you to wait on the doorstep when you could slip in and poke around." Burke would normally have bridled at the word 'spy' but, faced with Richard Fletcher's obvious enthusiasm and apparent goodwill, it was difficult to resent it. "I'm pleased to see that we stopped you before you saw anything, though. Proves that our attempts to keep our doings private seem to be working."

"Indeed they are." Burke favoured Fletcher with his most disarming smile. "But exactly what are these 'doings' you are so anxious to keep secret."

"Ah!" Fletcher had led Burke into what had obviously been designed one of the principle rooms of a private house but which was now clearly an office. He had already turned, apparently about to gesture Burke to a seat, but now he hesitated and looked at Burke appraisingly.

"You have been told nothing of my work."

"Nothing at all."

"But you are here to hunt out spies in our camp."

It was Burke's turn to pause. "You seem remarkably well informed."

Fletcher smiled. "I have the confidence of our commander-in-chief. Sir Arthur told me you would be here to assist us."

"My mission made no specific mention of you. Merely that there were concerns that some senior Portuguese officials were not, perhaps, entirely to be trusted."

"But to be trusted with what, Colonel Burke? What secrets could they betray? Their scouts know where our armies lie, licking their wounds since Talavera and, frankly, doing little else. The political intrigues of the government are known to all the tavern gossips in Lisbon and Marshal Beresford's reorganisation of the Portuguese army, worthy as it is, is hardly crucial intelligence. In any case it is, by its nature, known to practically every soldier in the country."

Burke suppressed a sigh. Once he, too, had thought spying might be a glamorous pursuit, tracking down some French villain with a despatch case full of documents labelled 'Top Secret'. Fifteen years acting as one of His Majesty's Confidential Agents had disabused him of such fanciful notions. "I fear that most espionage work is dull stuff, Colonel. A remark let slip in a tavern that suggests a regiment may be about to leave its quarters, a merchant who has taken orders for more supplies than the local forces usually use: all these unconsidered trifles can be combined to tell an experienced intelligencer when an army is moving. Details of the roads – and especially any news about the repair of roads or bridges – can tell us the likely direction of march. The local whores can provide a wealth of information about morale and doctors are distressingly prone to complain of the number of soldiers under their care. It's possible, of course, that there is a traitorous general or a conniving politician who can save us the trouble of collecting such trivia, but even there we would be dealing in the daily grind of military administration. I will find such a man, or men, if they exist but there will be no dramatic denouement to my work. As you say, what great secret could they betray?"

Fletcher stepped across to a table that dominated one side of the room. A cloth covered whatever documents had been left on it.

"I think I should show you this. It seems to me that sometimes those who work in the secret world can lose themselves in mysteries of their own creation."

He rolled back the cloth. Below was a map table, dominated by a map of the land north of Lisbon. Sketches of earthworks and fortifications were scattered around it.

Burke stepped forward to view it more closely. Two lines crossed the map from the Atlantic coast of Portugal to the river Tagus that ran north from Lisbon. The lines followed the crests of the hills north of the capital and separated Lisbon and its hinterland from the rest of the country.

It took a while for the enormity of what he was looking at to sink in.

"It makes Hadrian's wall look unambitious, doesn't it?" Fletcher's pride in the project was obvious in his voice.

Burke looked at one of the sketches. It was a plan for a small fort and carefully drawn arcs showed the area that would be covered from the three gun emplacements it housed.

Along the two lines shown on the map were hundreds of crosses, each one numbered. The sketch was numbered 40. Burke looked on the map. There was 40 – just South of the Alhandra-Bucellas road, some way to the north of Lisbon.

"You're planning to build Hadrian's wall but mount modern artillery on it!"

Fletcher grinned. It was the grin of a child who has found himself playing with toys from the biggest toybox in the world. "It's not actually a wall. The forts are placed along the contour line and each fort covers the approaches to itself and to the forts to either side. Here and there we will blast the ground in front of them so as to make the gradient artificially steeper, but generally the geography does the work for us. We don't need to build a wall when the Lord has provided one already."

"But the scale of such an enterprise! It looks very well on a map, but would anybody seriously plan to build it."

Fletcher's grin broadened. "We've already started."

Burke was sceptical. He had, it was true, been in Lisbon only a couple of days but he was sure that he would have had some inkling of a project of this magnitude. "After all, colonel," he pointed out, "you would need a regiment to make a serious start on this work."

"We're using Portuguese militia and civilian workers. Even when the lines are finished and manned, there will be little need for British troops. But I'm pleased that you struggle to believe me, for the Lines are the great secret we do not want the French to learn. Sir Arthur's whole strategy depends on the Lines and we don't want the Frogs anticipating our moves."

"But the Portuguese must know, if they are providing the labour, and the Portuguese, we believe, are not to be trusted."

"The Portuguese are fine people and utterly committed to the defeat of the French and their expulsion from their country." Fletcher was not grinning now. He was clearly angry at any suggestion of disloyalty amongst those working on his project. "There have been questions about some of the leaders of the army and of the government, but these are the rich and powerful and they see advantages to working with the French in the hope that they can save their wealth and grow their power. But the ordinary man here has no wealth and no power. All he has is his country and he will sacrifice everything to save it from the French."

"But the generals and the politicians can't be relied upon to keep your plans a secret."

"Which is why we don't tell them. It's why we are hidden away in this house, far from the other officers. It's why we work with the militia, who are lucky to get a uniform, food every couple of days and pay when there's cash left over after the army has taken its share. They hate the army. They can be relied upon not to talk about what they are doing."

"Does Beresford know?"

There was a glimpse of that grin again. "He knows that Sir Arthur has ordered the building of additional fortifications north of Lisbon. We've even sent him sketches of a couple of the forts, but he has no idea of the scale of the exercise. And he mustn't know. He's loyal, but he spends half his time with generals and politicians and he likes to impress. He can't keep a secret. His intentions are good, but he'll boast about the Lines and word will spread and …" He shrugged helplessly.

"Would that be such a problem? I mean, the French are in no position to stop your work. They're hundreds of miles away. And if they do try to occupy Lisbon again, they will see your defences for themselves. Is there some secret route through that we need to keep from them?"

"No, nothing like that. It's Sir Arthur's strategy that matters and, if they know of the existence of the Lines, they may work that out and then seek to frustrate it."

Burke looked again at the map. The Lines were about 30 miles north of Lisbon, much further than made any sense for the defence of the city. They cut off the whole of the peninsula that Lisbon was built on. Within the Lines was not only the city but hundreds of square miles of farmland. "He's going to pull his whole Army behind the Lines and over-winter here."

Fletcher nodded. "And he's going to bring the civilian population with him. Everything north of Torres Vedras is to be abandoned. The windmills will be destroyed. The villages will, as far as possible, be made uninhabitable. Any food that can't be transported within the Lines will be burned. North of Torres Vedras will be a desert."

Burke nodded. He knew the way the French army lived off the land. If they pursued the British as far as the Lines, they would find themselves unable to move forward and without the food they would need to survive.

"You see the point," said Fletcher. "If they understand the plan, they may attempt to outflank our forces and cut off our retreat through the

Lines. Since Talavera they have been able to field more troops than us. It's one approach they might well try. Failing that, they let us go and they over-winter in Spain. They'll probably end up better fed than us and come spring they can again muster more men than us. Remember that Napoleon has introduced conscription. The French can summon up as many more men as they want and march their reinforcements down across the Pyrenees. Wellington has to beg for every man he wants before Parliament might reluctantly put a few on a ship to make its way from England. Sir Arthur will leave his withdrawal until the last possible minute and then limp westward, trusting that the French will follow him. And then we wait and watch them starve."

CHAPTER 5: Winning hearts and minds

It was a short walk back to Snr Lopez's house. The grid plan of the new part of the city meant that Burke did not have to think about the route and he found himself making his way without paying any attention to his surroundings. Instead his thoughts centred on Fletcher's plans and the importance of keeping them secret from the French. Suddenly, instead of a vague mission to look out for potential subversives amongst the Portuguese, he had to protect a secret that could be vital to the war. But how to do that? He knew now what secret needed protecting from French spies, but as to who those spies might be, he had no idea at all. So far, there was no indication that Fletcher's secrets had been exposed to the enemy. Indeed, the French were probably unaware that there was a secret to expose. So did they have agents close to the government and ready to betray their country? And how could you begin to find them?

At least when he arrived at his temporary home he found a message from Beresford. The general was to meet with some of his Portuguese allies to discuss their concerns about the behaviour of British troops in the capital. He would be obliged if Colonel Burke were to join him.

The meeting was to take place that afternoon. Most of Lisbon's inhabitants would be enjoying their postprandial siesta, but Beresford, typically, had paid no regard to local custom. Burke could only be grateful that Lisbon was still quite cool and that he would not be suffering the heat of summer.

Burke arrived promptly. Beresford was there and did not keep him waiting more than a couple of minutes, but there was no sign of the Portuguese who had asked for the meeting.

"Typical," grumbled Beresford. "You can never trust these fellows to turn up on time."

Burke was amused to note that Beresford's obvious dislike for the Portuguese meant that he appeared, for the moment, to have forgotten how much he disliked Burke.

They sat a while in silence, Beresford looking up every couple of minutes at the tall case clock in a corner of the room.

"Look here," he said after almost ten minutes had passed, "I don't need to stay for this. Get my clerk to find you another room and have them shown there. They insisted on speaking to me but, if they can't be on time, they'll have to settle for you. You're a senior officer. You'll do."

"Do you have any particular message you wish to convey?"

Beresford shook his head. "Just listen to them as politely as you can manage and assure them that you will convey their concerns to me and I will take action."

"Will you?"

"Of course not. Unless it's simple and obvious, in which case you can deal with it. Otherwise promise them whatever you want, usher them out of the office, and you need never think about it again. That's half of what my liaison officers do."

"And the other half?"

"Chase the lazy buggers when they've not done whatever we've asked them to do. You'll get the hang of it soon enough." He waved a gesture of dismissal. "Now see my clerk and find a room or they'll turn up while you're still here and I'll end up having to talk to them."

Burke wasted no time in leaving. This would be his first opportunity to meet any of the men (he was confident that they would all be men) who were as close as Portugal came to a government.

He need not have hurried. The clerk found him a room and, after five minutes, returned to offer him a glass of wine while he waited. He sipped at the wine for another ten minutes before the clerk knocked to announce the arrival of Snr Morais and Snr Carvalho.

The two men who entered were young – younger than Burke. They were smartly dressed. As far as Burke could judge, they seemed to have spent an inordinate amount of money on their clothes and they wore them with the haughtiness of men who knew themselves to be better than you and who had chosen their wardrobe to demonstrate the fact. The younger man was even wearing a wig, which Burke regarded as a ridiculous affectation for anyone under the age of forty who was not at a formal occasion. Burke despised the two of them on sight, but he was glad that William had made sure his uniform was as smart as anything a mere civilian could muster.

"Where is Marshal Beresford?" the older man demanded. "And who the hell are you?"

Burke was inclined to call him out for his arrogance. He knew Wellington disapproved of duelling, but surely he would make an exception in these circumstances? He bit the inside of his cheek until the temptation had passed. He needed to get to know the potential traitors and if these two weren't betraying their country, it seemed likely that the people he needed to investigate were part of their social set. Born into the aristocracy and growing up expecting to be part of court life, they were just too young to have been selected to sail off with the Prince Regent when he fled Lisbon for Brazil. Now, slighted (in their view) by their monarch, they were slighted again by the British. Being young, their response was anger and bluster. Being older, Burke recognised the value of a more subtle approach.

"My name is Colonel Burke," he said. "I'm terribly sorry that Marshal Beresford was unable to meet you, but he was unfortunately called away on urgent business. But you must be hot after dragging yourself all this way in the sun. May I offer you some wine?"

The clerk was summoned and more wine appeared.

They did not unbend enough to thank him for the wine, treating it instead as an automatic courtesy to somebody of their importance. Still, they seemed marginally less hostile.

They had come, they said, to complain that many of the British troops were behaving inappropriately. They insulted young ladies. They stole from stall holders. "They behave," said the older man, "more like an occupying army than like the soldiers of an ally."

James nodded sympathetically and poured Snr Morais another drink. He looked to Burke as if he was in his late thirties, though the curly hair made him look younger. Perhaps that was why he was so aggressive. Perhaps he felt that people did not take him as seriously as he clearly thought they should, dismissing him as a pretty boy.

Burke turned towards Carvalho, topping up his glass. There was no danger that Carvalho had ever been seen as a pretty boy. Burke thought of the way that some women would befriend much more attractive members of their sex, benefitting, they felt, from their proximity to beauty. Of course, any benefit they might obtain was paid for with their benefactor's casual assumption of their acolyte's unquestioning loyalty. Carvalho's role at this meeting was, it seemed, to nod enthusiastically at every tedious point Morais made and occasionally, when the older man paused for breath, to repeat the last point he had made, in case Burke had not paid Morais proper attention.

Burke listened to everything said to him, his face a mask of civility. He made a point of writing extensive notes, although he had an excellent memory. He wrote slowly and the two men drank more wine as he did.

After almost an hour, the meeting drew to an end with Burke promising that he would speak to Marshal Beresford and ensure that something was done. In fact he had no intention of speaking to Beresford. It would be a complete waste of time anyway. He would, though, have a word with Sgt Brown who would in turn have a word with other NCOs in Lisbon and things would improve, at least for a while. It was, as Burke knew very well, the NCOs and not the generals who were responsible for the day-to-day running of the Army.

By the time the two men left, a little bit drunk and assured that Beresford's representative understood their importance, they may not have been exactly friendly, but their attitudes certainly seemed to be mellowing. Burke could only hope that the mellowness did not entirely wear off once they were sober.

* * *

In the end, it was as easy as that. A sympathetic hearing, a glass of wine, the occasional good result: that was all that was needed to take the first steps to gaining the trust of the aristocracy. Word spread of the sympathetic Englishman and gradually he began to meet more of them. People started to ask to meet with Colonel Burke rather than Marshal Beresford and if Beresford noticed the change, he must simply have welcomed the reduction in his workload. Certainly he never complained about it. In fact, he unbent enough to invite Burke to a couple of the dinners held in the castle. Here the general sat in state at the head of the table, while local officials and a few men like Morais and Carvalho were condescended to in the interests of improving

Anglo-Portuguese relations. Burke would usually be placed between a merchant and a baron. Barons, he knew, were two-a-penny in Lisbon and his placement was clearly Beresford's way of showing that he was still not forgiven.

Burke didn't care about the snub. The food was good, though Beresford made no concessions to the local cuisine, insisting on what he called "decent English fare", by which he meant roast beef. It must have been a challenge to the local firm that had the connections to handle all of Beresford's formal catering, but they did an impressive job. And even if he was never sat with representatives of the more senior aristocracy, Burke felt a baron was a good place to start. He found social settings valuable in his line of work. Wine made people indiscrete and indiscretions were the stock in trade of a professional spy.

Burke flattered and amused at these dinners, displaying the charm that he could always summon up when needed. That, combined with his successes in calming angry petitioners to Beresford's office, meant he found himself invited to occasional social events on his own account.

Now he finally felt that he had something to report to Gordon. So far it was only gossip, but gossip is the base currency of a spy and he needed to have something to show for his time in Lisbon.

His first report explained that many of the aristocrats were unconvinced of the virtue of the British cause. Their resentment of a ruler who had abandoned them when he fled to Brazil transferred itself to what they saw as the new rulers headed by Beresford. Most of them, Burke wrote, posed no real threat. They were grumbling, as people always grumble when governments impose new regulations. Portugal was, after all, at war and Beresford's rule must inevitably have sometimes appeared harsh.

There were those, though, who were sympathetic to the French cause and prepared to toast Napoleon and his armies. This looked more like treason, but it was difficult to blame them when entire regiments of the Portuguese army had switched sides *en masse*. There were many in Lisbon who had close personal friends now serving under Napoleon. Masséna, currently leading the French facing Wellington, had the Portuguese 3rd Marquis of Alorna as one of his staff officers. It was unfortunate, and to be discouraged, but Burke suggested that mass arrests were impractical as well as doing no good at all to Portuguese morale.

Finally, he suspected that there were those who would, given the opportunity, actively work against British interests. William, busy ciphering his message, suggested that if he could provide those names, they could go home.

"Precisely." Burke was not amused. "But until then, William, it appears that we are going to have to keep working."

Gordon replied in cypher, which must have annoyed Beresford who, Burke was certain, had attempted to intercept it. Burke was to provide a list of names provisionally sorted into the categories he had identified and continue to investigate those he deemed the most serious risk.

So Burke continued to deal with the litany of complaints that covered everything from the noise of regimental bands to the number of soldiers on the streets on the Sabbath when, surely, they should have been in church or in their quarters contemplating the state of their souls.

After a while, Burke found that he was enjoying the work. As the young aristocrats grew to trust him, they came less often with confected demands, designed only to show the English as uncaring and themselves as the champions of their people. Instead they made considered requests, which Burke found satisfaction in dealing with.

An early issue was concerned with payment for supplies to the Army. Wellington had given firm orders that the Army was to pay for anything supplied by the locals and Beresford was strict in ensuring that they did so. He was less careful, though, in setting appropriate levels of payment. Vegetables were paid at a standard rate per pound, whatever kind of vegetable and whatever the quality. The price set naturally assumed the cheapest vegetables of the worst quality. In theory, locals could refuse to sell at these derisory prices, but faced with an officer from the Commissariat supported by three or four burly infantrymen, it could be difficult to refuse their offer. Burke decided against raising the issue with Beresford, but instead went directly to the offices of the Commissariat. He let it be known that his reports would go directly to Wellington (an exaggeration, but far from a lie) and left them to decide for themselves what action, if any, to take. Over the next few weeks, according to his Portuguese visitors, more reasonable prices were offered.

That feat did actually take some real effort, but Burke was surprised how simple it was to solve many of the problems. The concerns about soldiers disturbing the peace of the Sabbath were particularly easily dealt with. He had a quiet word with commanding officers suggesting that Wellington will be disappointed to hear that many of the men were failing to attend church parade. (He doubted this was true but nobody was going to argue.) Another series of chats with regimental chaplains suggesting that they spend longer on their sermons at church parade (an idea that obviously appealed to them) and the problem was, if not solved, at least considerably ameliorated.

As Burke spent more time with the men who considered themselves the natural leaders of Portuguese society, he found himself increasingly sympathetic to them. They were, he felt, more pathetic than threatening. While they remained a privileged class who were, in theory, responsible for all the most important offices of state – administrative, judicial, political and military – everyone knew that they were the ones not quite important enough to be considered worth taking to Brazil. Left behind in Portugal, they now found that administration and military control were both now the responsibility of the English and political power, in a country torn by war and with its government in exile, was a chimera. They had no political power and they knew it.

Most of those who came to Burke with their complaints were, at least at first glance, like Morais and Carvalho. They were young – or at best middle-aged. The older aristocrats – the ones who had money and could exercise real power – were all in Brazil. The men left to deal with the English in Portugal disguised their awareness of their insignificance with an overweening arrogance that, after a while, Burke found amusing rather than annoying. He remembered his youth in Ireland: the constant resentment of the English who failed to acknowledge the status that he should be accorded as the son of a landlord. His response had been to step away from his past, losing his accent, renouncing his Catholicism and committing himself to work with the English who, he knew, held his country in contempt. It was harder for these young men to accept reality. They had, after all, much more to lose: generations of wealth and power that left its mark, however much the wealth had been dissipated and however much the power had dwindled away. They did not have the strength that would be needed to break away from these backgrounds. Yet, even as he dismissed their pretensions as foolish, part of him admired their determination to cling to the trappings of their old positions for as long as possible.

The men he dealt with recognised his sympathy, even if he took care to disguise his pity. He began to find that, when he was required to pass on some order from Beresford (though he took care to phrase it as a request), they would try to help, sometimes even without being reminded. Occasionally there would even be grudging praise for the British efforts on behalf of their country.

With the growing trust between Burke and the local aristocracy, he found himself regularly invited to socialise with them. Relaxing with his new friends, Burke would sometimes mention his Irish past. Although he was never so obvious as to attack the English, he would let slip from time to time that he understood what it was like to have an English army occupying your country. As word spread of the attitudes of this unlikely English officer with his Irish background and his sympathy for the Portuguese, so he was invited to more gatherings.

Burke spoke Spanish like a native and Portuguese, he felt, was not that different. After a few weeks he was already on his way to being fluent in the language. He was an amusing and pleasant guest and soon he was out with local friends two or three times a week.

Generally the invitations were to drinks parties or soirees where daughters entertained the guests with performances on the pianoforte or singing or, if the host was feeling particularly unkind, both. Occasionally, though, some of the gentlemen would cluster together and politics would be discussed. James Burke was not encouraged to join these discussions and if he did happen to drift towards one of the groups it would turn out that what they were discussing was the weather or the likely outcome of a horse race. It was usually the likely outcome of a horse race, for the Portuguese aristocracy were obsessed with horses. You could, in England, be a poor rider but a duke, and hence be accounted amongst the highest in society. In Portugal, if you were not a good rider, your aristocratic rank was no help: you were practically a nobody. Burke, fortunately, was a good enough horseman to join in these conversations and gradually people relaxed around him. Sometimes they would complain about the English and someone would look nervously in his direction but then there would be a joke about his Irish past and they would relax again. They did, however, draw the line at discussing their attitudes to the French in front of him.

This could not, in Burke's opinion, go on. Pleasant as it was to socialise with these young men, who were not so bad once you got to know them, the whole point of the exercise was to establish how prepared they were to assist the French. So the next time that Napoleon's troops were mentioned, Burke decided to share some more about his past.

"Say what you like about the French, they make damn good soldiers. I served with them myself before they were at war with England."

This generated, to put it mildly, a degree of surprise among the other guests. Burke had to explain that there had been no shame in fighting for the French when he was a young man and England and France were not at war. "There was an entire regiment made up of British soldiers, mostly from Ireland. The Regiment of Dillon, it was called." Somehow, though he was speaking in Portuguese, he managed to suffuse the last statement with more than a touch of Irish brogue.

Once his audience had got over the initial shock, they bombarded him with questions. Had he trained in Paris? Yes, he had trained as an officer at the Ecole Militaire. Had he fought? Yes, in the West Indies. Then came questions about the campaigns he had fought in and the quality of the French soldiers. He answered them all honestly but pointed out that much had changed since those days. "There was no Napoleon back then."

By now he was the centre of an excited group, all anxious to know more about his experiences. When somebody asked if he thought Napoleon had made big changes to the French army, it seemed the most natural thing in the world and he was happy to reply. Napoleon, he explained, had brought considerable improvements, mainly by appointing new and better officers. The main way he had achieved this was by appointing on merit, rather than reserving the best positions for members of the aristocracy, but Burke tactfully refrained from mentioning this. There were organisational changes too and some changes in the way the army fought. "The French now march faster than they used to. Their regular pace is higher than any other army in Europe. It makes them incredibly manoeuvrable and Napoleon takes full advantage of that. And the Emperor qualified as an artillery officer so now the French usually go into battle with more artillery support than most armies and they use their cannon with great skill."

From this to a general discussion of Napoleon and the French was a short step. Now, after weeks of cultivating his new friends, Burke was finally hearing their honest feelings about the French.

That many of the Portuguese aristocracy – or certainly those living in Lisbon – had quite a positive view of the French came as no great surprise. They thought of themselves as men of the world, living in what they regarded as Europe's most important port with its trade links to the Americas, England and the Mediterranean. They felt Portugal, with the Catholic church still holding so much power, had somehow missed out on the Enlightenment. Things had improved in the 1700s with a new reforming Prime Minister but all that had stopped when Queen Maria had ascended the throne determined, in their view, to turn back the clock. Napoleon had got rid of an outdated monarchy, slashed the rights of the Church and encouraged advances in science. Admittedly some of the aristocracy had suffered, but many continued to prosper and the Emperor was creating new marquises and dukes and even princes on a regular basis. France was leading the way into a rational, unified Europe, looking forward and outward while Portugal, they felt, was looking back towards a glorious past and rejecting what the 19th century had to offer.

"So how do you feel about the English in all this?"

The English weren't bad, most agreed, but several remarked that London was not a particularly loyal friend to Portugal. The English had been slow to come to their country's aid when the French first invaded and when they finally drove them out for the first time they signed a treaty which allowed the French to take with them all the loot they had stolen from the Portuguese during their occupation. "I lost all the wine from my vineyards in the north. The French stole it and the

English allowed them to take it away. They even provided ships to carry it."

There was a lot of grumbling agreement. Unlike the aristocrats living in the north of the country who, Burke knew, had often seen their homes plundered, the gentlemen of Lisbon had not been pillaged in the same way but those with agricultural interests in the areas that the French had occupied had lost crops and livestock. "They started by taking what they needed to feed their army but then they just helped themselves to anything they thought they could take back to France and sell at a profit." Those who had country homes and who had been foolish enough to leave their wives' jewels there lost those, of course.

"I had my statues stolen," said one. Really? People were surprised. It seemed unlikely. No, explained Burke, it was not unlikely at all. "Napoleon is collecting artworks from all over Europe and putting them all on display in a great museum in Paris." He didn't tell them how he knew. There was no reason they should ever learn that he had been in Paris only a few months ago. "You should be flattered really. He only steals the best."

From then on, Burke was seen as a man they could trust. He would never share their darkest secrets – he was a British officer after all – but he was included in their discussions and soon learned a great deal about how it might be possible for some of the leading lights of Portuguese society to have thrown their lot in with the French. It was not that they were betraying their country but caught in a war between Britain and France – a war that was not of their making – it was not at all clear why they should favour one side or the other. For those in the north, who had direct experience of the worst of French excesses, the choice was usually clear, but for the people of Lisbon, where French troops had been kept on a short leash by their commanders, the choice between British and French was not that straightforward.

Burke began to make notes on the people he met and produced reports that he passed back to Gordon. He still thought that most of those who complained about the British posed no threat, but it was the business of a confidential agent to provide lists of potential spies and he was diligent in his work.

Not everyone could be dismissed as casually. After one party that had proved unusually raucous for Lisbon, a group of young bloods had started to sing La Marseillaise. Even Napoleon had banned the song as the French national anthem, judging it too revolutionary in tone. Burke noted the names of the impromptu choristers and their names were added to a list of men who might pose a serious threat. Not, Burke thought, that serious. While they might be carried away with radical ideas when drunk, it seemed unlikely that they would do more than produce the odd pamphlet. Whether they were just fundamentally too loyal to their monarch to rebel openly, or maybe too lazy or cowardly, he did not know and nor did he care. He had spent enough time in the company of revolutionaries to consider he had a fine instinct for that sort of thing.

He did not have to worry about those who were most committed to the French cause. They had worked actively with the French during the occupation and had, probably wisely, decided to leave Portugal as the French withdrew. They were in no position to spy for Napoleon now.

That left a few who he considered might well be prepared to help the French but had not chosen to come out openly to work with them. Men who nodded approvingly when La Marseillaise was sung, but who had been careful not to join in. Or men like Snr Silva, who had drunk rather too much at one party and suggested that he was closer to the French than he ought to have been. He had been there with his friend Bernardo Moutinho, who had hurried to change the subject. Best, Burke thought, to put Moutinho on the list too.

Dom Costa had taken him aside once and started to talk to him about his work for Beresford. Although Burke had made his job sound as boring as possible, Costa had claimed it sounded fascinating and had bombarded him with questions. Costa was added to the list.

Burke could never be sure, of course. Perhaps Costa had only been being polite. Perhaps João Patricio, who demonstrated an encyclopaedic knowledge of Portuguese military dispositions, was innocently interested in military matters – although he had no connections with the army at all.

He looked at his potential spies carefully, particularly checking to see if any of them had a relationship with some of the traitors who had fled the country. It was obvious that the aristocracy was cliquey. Well, Burke thought, that really went without saying – they were aristocrats, after all. Even so, the web of relationships, based on blood, regional links, political affiliations or simple personal affection, meant that it was not easy to work out who could be relied on to be loyal and who were potential traitors.

In the end he came up with a list of a dozen names, including Morais and Carvalho.

Many of those on the list might be entirely guiltless. At the same time there might be a spy who concealed himself amongst those professing complete loyalty to their British allies. Perhaps somebody he had dismissed as lazy or cowardly was, in fact, cunning. And maybe there was no spy at all. Still, if there were a spy, he felt it was more than likely to be one of those twelve.

The names were handed to William Brown who carefully transcribed them into cipher and they made their way to Gordon's office in Horse Guards.

It was not enough, of course.

"It's tittle-tattle," he complained to William.

"Maybe not worth the time I spent ciphering it."

James hurried to reassure William that his efforts had not been wasted. "It's all grist to Gordon's mill. There's always a chance that one of those names is known to him from someone else's work. In any case, if the worst comes to the worst, he can always arrange to have them all arrested. It would be nice to have something more concrete to offer him, though."

"And how do you intend to do that?"

"I think I might start by paying another call on Colonel Fletcher."

* * *

This time he took care to write to Fletcher in advance and to wait at the door until he was invited in. He had no wish to stand in the hallway with a hostile guard pointing a pistol at his vitals again.

The colonel was in his office with more plans scattered across the table.

"Every one different," he said as Burke looked at them. "Each exactly fitted to the ground available and the field of fire required.

When it's finished every inch of land from the Atlantic to the Tagus will be covered by cannon fire."

Burke looked duly impressed. He didn't have to fake his interest: the whole idea was almost beyond imagination.

"What if they try to cross the Tagus?"

"We've dammed some of the streams there so that the whole area is turned to marsh."

"Difficult to cross but not impossible."

"I know." Fletcher's face lit up with another of his boyish grins. "That's why we're putting gunships on the river. They'll be under cannon fire all the time they're stuck in the marsh."

Burke nodded, impressed. Fletcher, it seemed, had thought of everything.

"It's fascinating, but not why I came. Have you had any more concerns about spies."

"Nothing at all. But we're doing more building now. That means more men. The forts are being built mainly from material on site: they're basically earthworks faced with stone where it's needed so there's not an obvious amount of building material being sent north. But anybody who's tried to buy a spade lately might work out that somebody is doing an awful lot of digging. And there's food and officers running to and fro to check on progress."

"Have you had any dealings with any of these men? Or had any of them showing particular interest in what you're doing here?"

Fletcher frowned as he looked through the list. "No, none of these mean anything to me. Do you think they are your spies?"

Burke shook his head. "They're just people I want to know more about. They could be shining repositories of virtue. In fact one or two of them probably are. But maybe one or two aren't."

Fletcher took one more glance at the list before handing it back to Burke. "I'm sorry I can't help," he said. And then, as Burke left, "Good hunting."

* * *

If none of the names meant anything to Fletcher, the next step was to bring William into play. His sergeant had so far had little to do, other than look after his uniform and if he spent any more time brushing it there was a real danger that he would wear out the fabric.

William had many skills that made him an excellent spy. He was a top-class forger, he understood invisible inks and could make them from everyday household materials, his skills with a needle and thread meant he could sew secret messages into anything from a jacket to a saddle and leave no sign that he had been there, he was a dab hand with a picklock. But probably his single greatest skill was his ability to charm the women of the servants' quarters and quietly learn most of what there was to know about a household.

"Do you want me to start with anybody in particular?"

"I'm afraid not, William. It could be any of them or none of them. It might take a while."

William smiled. "It will be my pleasure," he said.

* * *

For over a week, nothing happened. Burke continued to liaise with the local aristocracy by day and socialise with them by night. William would vanish every evening and return late at night or early in the morning. James did not ask him for daily reports on progress. Once there was something to report, he knew that Sgt Brown would tell him all there was to tell. Until then he was happy not to hear all the details. Brown was a married man and James liked his wife. What he didn't know he didn't have to feel guilty about.

It was towards the middle of the second week that William woke him with a cup of tea (he took his role as servant very seriously) and reported on progress to date.

"Those two blokes who turned up demanding the general when you started this caper …"

"Snrs Morais and Carvalho."

"Yeh, them. Thick as thieves they are."

"They're close, yes. This is old news, William."

"Well they go out drinking together."

"That's not that usual, I know. Most of that class do their drinking in each other's houses. But is it suspicious?"

"It is when you know where they drink."

Burke raised an interrogative eyebrow.

"*A Tendinha*."

"'The Tent'. Should I have heard of it?"

"No, sir, you shouldn't. And that's the point. It's a rough sort of a place over in the Alfama." Alfama, Burke had learned, was the name given to the older parts of town built under the castle rock. He quite liked it but it was not the sort of area he would expect to bump into people like Morais and Carvalho.

"How often do they go?"

"Most weeks. Usually on a Tuesday."

"Well unless we come up with a better idea over the next few days, I imagine we will be drinking at *A Tendinha* on Tuesday."

CHAPTER 6: An evening at 'A Tendinha'

Burke could hardly turn up in his uniform. Besides the fact that he didn't want to be recognised, *A Tendinha* wasn't the sort of place anyone would expect to see an English colonel drinking. Burke could probably have passed himself off as Portuguese, but he wasn't sure that his accent and knowledge of local ways would fool his fellow drinkers that he came from Lisbon. Better to go with William and the two of them could play the part of drinking companions while keeping an eye on what was passing in the bar.

William's Portuguese was coming along nicely, but he lacked Burke's natural ability to pick up languages and there was no question of him sounding like a local. Basically, if he was going to admit to being English, it was most natural that he was a soldier, so the two of them decided to be soldiers together.

Burke spent the next few days hiding away in his room while his normally immaculate hair was cut terrifyingly badly by William. "Don't worry, sir. I'll be able to trim it back afterwards and you'll look as tidy as ever." Burke looked at himself in the mirror, shuddered, and prayed William was right.

By Tuesday morning, his stubble was itchy, his fingernails were filthy and his air of unkempt grubbiness was uncomfortably convincing. William had acquired a uniform that he tossed carelessly on the bed. Burke picked it up gingerly.

"This looks so worn that there has to be a decent chance of it falling apart over the course of the evening."

William grinned. "In that case you'd best wear clean underwear."

Burke noticed a dark stain on the breast where a hole had been crudely darned.

"William, was the last person to wear this shot?"

William shrugged. "I didn't ask, sir. Best not think too much about it."

William's own choice of clothing did not look anything like as disreputable. He'd found a shabby uniform from somewhere that lacked his sergeant's chevrons and he was unusually slovenly, but otherwise not much changed. It made sense, Burke thought. Morais and Carvalho had never met Sgt Brown so a disguise was not necessary. The changes in his own appearance would not fool anyone who was paying him attention, but he should not be recognised so long as he was just one of the customers in the background.

People ate late in Lisbon and Brown, who had spent a fair few evenings out drinking ("and by way of business as you wanted me getting to know people") confirmed that the place would be practically empty until ten.

"We'll arrive soon after that," Burke said. People were less likely to notice you if you were already established somewhere – part of the scenery, so to speak – than if you arrived after them.

* * *

Well before ten thirty, they were settled at a table towards the back of *A Tendinha*. Tucked away as it was, it still gave them a good view of the door. As the place got busier it was harder to see everything that was going on through the crush of people but Burke was happy that they would be able to keep track of Morais and Carvalho if they turned up.

While they waited, they talked about Talavera. They had to talk about something – sitting in silence would draw attention – and Talavera was a natural thing to talk about. Anybody who had been there that day had a story and they all seemed compelled to tell it to anybody who was prepared to listen. Burke had heard all of William's stories before, of course, but he still found himself gripped by them. He felt obscurely guilty for not having been there.

William made light of the horror but there was an edge to his voice when he told those stories: Peters staring at his leg in disbelief as a cannonball neatly removed his foot, Wilkins struggling to stand as he fired volley after volley with the blood seeping from the wound in his leg, the Guards breaking and the French so close to taking the hill.

"But then we beat the buggers, sir. It was a famous victory."

"A famous victory indeed."

But both men were thinking of the retreat that had followed that 'victory'. The men who had starved, collapsed and died; the wounded who had been abandoned. Burke had been there for that and the retreat had been bad enough even though he had missed the battle.

Neither of them really believed it had been a victory.

They were so caught up in their stories – Burke never found it boring, however often he heard it – that they nearly missed Morais making his way in. Carvalho was close behind him.

The place was packed by now but as soon as the two aristocrats had decided on their table, the men sitting there stood, knuckling their foreheads and moving away.

Burke moved around the table to get a better view.

"See anything?" asked William, who couldn't see from where he was sitting.

"Two men drinking wine. It's odd, given the quality of the wine here and what they are used to at home, but it's not anything illegal."

"It's not that bad," said William, looking meaningfully at his empty glass.

Burke caught the eye of the serving girl and more wine appeared. "I'd prefer beer, but you get used to this stuff." William took a healthy swig.

"Don't let it go to your head. There may yet be something to make the evening worthwhile."

For half an hour nothing at all happened. Even sipping as slowly as they could, James and William finished their wine and had to order another or risk drawing attention to themselves. Burke took the opportunity to pay for a drink for the waitress. It never hurt, in his view, to have a potential friend around, especially if you were drinking in a place like *A Tendinha.*

The wine had arrived when Burke saw a young man enter the tavern. He was wearing the broad hat and jacket favoured by the locals and Burke was hardly paying him any attention as he pushed his way through the crowd. When he headed straight for the table where Morais and Carvalho were sitting, though, he lost all interest in the wine.

He could not hear what was being said over the noise of the crowd, but he saw Morais gesture to a man at the next table who obediently gave up his seat so that his stool could be pushed across for the newcomer to join the two aristocrats.

They made an unlikely trio. Morais and Carvalho had dressed down for the evening – no ruffs at the front of their waistcoats, no gold thread, shoes that were designed more for walking than to impress. Even so they were clearly aristocrats. Their companion, though, looked like a regular working man – the sort of person that the likes of Morais would not normally allow themselves to be seen in conversation with. Yet here were the three of them, heads bent forwards, talking earnestly together.

They spoke for about five minutes and then Morais passed something to the young man. For a moment the candlelight glinted on a coin before the money vanished into the man's waistcoat and he rose to his feet, bowed slightly to his companions, turned and headed directly out of the tavern.

"Shall I follow him."

"Not now, William. They show no sign of leaving. I think there is more to learn here."

Burke was right. Soon another stranger entered and the little drama was repeated.

This time, as he left, William followed while Burke sat and watched the scene played out for a third time.

Nothing, he decided, would be gained by staying. If the two suspects (for by now they definitely were suspects) stayed on, he would only see a repetition of what had taken place so far. It would be more useful to follow the third man and see what he could learn of him.

As the man left, Burke was behind him. He left a sensible distance, confident that the man would have no idea he was being followed. Burke had, after all, done this often enough to be sure of his abilities.

What caught him out was the warren of alleys that made up Alfama. This was the area he had explored when he followed the fishmonger on his first walk around the city. He had found it difficult to navigate even by daylight. In the dark, he struggled to work out where he was. The streets were so narrow that anyone glancing over their shoulder could easily see if they were being followed, so he had to fall further behind than he was comfortable with. Despite that, he stayed with his quarry for a quarter of a mile before he turned one corner twenty paces behind the stranger and found the path ahead empty.

A few yards in was an alley even narrower than the others. Burke relaxed. The man must have headed down there. But as he was about to turn into the rancid smelling passage, he noticed a patch of darkness a few yards further down on the other side. It was another alley.

The first or the second? Or had he perhaps slipped through one of the doorways into whatever tenement he lived in. Ahead, he heard the sound of men drinking in a bar which, from its location, he imagined must be even less salubrious than *A Tendinha*. Perhaps he had made it that far and was now lost among the men drinking there.

Burke hesitated, looking first one way and then another. He could take one direction at random and trust to luck, but he knew that the chances of finding his man again were slim to non-existent. It was far more likely that he would run into a footpad in this maze of alleyways and getting stabbed in a random attack seemed a foolish risk to take.

He shrugged and set off for home. He hoped that at least his sergeant had had more success.

* * *

When he arrived back in his room, Brown was already there.

"Sorry, sir. I lost him. There was a group of blokes, well drunk, crowded out of a tavern and – well, you know how narrow those alleys are. By the time I've pushed past them, he's away."

"See if you can liberate some brandy from Snr Lopez's cellar. We'll make it up to him tomorrow, but now I think we both need a drink – and I can't face wine after the muck at *A Tendinha*."

Brown vanished away and returned after a few minutes clutching a bottle and two glasses.

For a while the two men drank together in silence. Then: "Are we going to try again, sir."

"I think we have to, William. Those meetings in *A Tendinha* aren't much to go on but they are all we've got." He took another thoughtful swig of brandy. "It might be worth getting more familiar with Alfama, though. It gives us a better chance of keeping up if we know the geography."

CHAPTER 7: A damsel in distress

The next morning found them climbing up towards the castle, branching off into side streets, exploring the alleys and getting a feel for the place. It was definitely an area inhabited by the labouring classes, but there was no obvious evidence of poverty. The people who lived here were dock workers and fishermen and there were thriving businesses to serve them. Some of the houses, small as they were, somehow fitted in workshops producing finely carved woodwork. Most of the locals probably bought their food from the stalls at the grand plaza of the new town, but there were plenty of shops selling fruit and vegetables for those who did not want to make the journey down to the waterfront and back again. There were, as Burke had already discovered, plenty of places to buy fish and their smell added to the various stenches produced in an area packed with houses and served by a sewage system which, such as it was, had seen little change since medieval times.

Despite the stink, Burke thought it was a pleasant enough place. The people seemed friendly, particularly as they neared the fort. William and him were both wearing the same disreputable uniforms as the night before, which seemed well suited to a casual stroll around the neighbourhood. They passed easily as just another couple of off-duty soldiers and it was obvious that a whole industry had grown up to cater for men just like they appeared to be. There were a few women hanging around a bit too obviously in doorways – though not many, for the city's Catholicism had survived the expulsion of the Jesuits and public lewdness was uncommon.

William stopped outside one bar and sniffed the air. "That's beer or I'm a Dutchman," he said. "Would you believe it – real beer."

Burke sniffed too. "I doubt it's very good beer, William. I think it's best avoided."

They moved around the corner – Alfama seemed nothing but corners – to see a young woman seated in a doorway sketching one of a group of soldiers lounging in the street. Next to her there was a sign in English: 'Your Picture While You Wait.'

"The spirit of enterprise at work, William. There have been British troops in Lisbon just two years and already the locals are making every provision for their entertainment."

It seemed, though, that her customer's friends were not satisfied with the quality of the entertainment being provided – or perhaps they misunderstood exactly what the girl was selling. They were making a series of suggestions that were becoming increasingly obscene. Glancing at William, Burke could see that even he was shocked by some of them.

The girl either did not understand what was being said, or chose to pretend not to. Her face was impassive as she sketched the man in front of her. Her lack of response, far from calming the men down, seemed to aggravate them.

"You going to let her ignore you like that, Johnny?"

Johnny was apparently the soldier having his portrait drawn and he turned towards his comrades and leered. "Let 'er finish me picture first."

"You 'ave to keep still, mister."

It was all the excuse Johnny needed. "I don't have to do anything for you, you tart."

Whether or not she understood the words, the girl clearly understood the tone. "Sit still or I not finish picture."

Burke wondered afterwards if Johnny might have let it go at that point but his friends saw the chance of sport and demanded that he "stand up for himself".

"You won't be spoken to like that, will you Johnny?"

"Show the little whore who's boss."

Johnny hesitated and then stepped across to the girl and turned to see the drawing.

"That's crap."

Burke and William had moved closer while things got messier and they were now close enough for Burke to see that the sketch was surprisingly good. He wasn't there as an art critic though. Provided things did not turn ugly, he had no intention of getting involved.

Johnny snatched the drawing from its easel and tore it in two.

The girl had made the mistake of stepping forward to try to save it and now he grabbed towards her. She pulled back, but not fast enough to stop him grabbing a handful of the embroidered bodice that she wore over her blouse.

There was the sound of ripping and the girl screamed. After that, in Burke's view, everything that followed was almost inevitable.

Johnny's friends, who up till then had been happy as spectators, goading him on, now felt they needed to join in. The sound of a woman screaming seemed to release some atavistic instinct in them and they moved forward as a mob.

"I think we might have to show an interest, William."

"I thought you'd never ask, sir."

The two stepped forward, Burke shouting in his best officer's voice: "Let her go and step away."

For a moment, the men responded automatically to the voice of authority. Then they looked at the two shabbily dressed men without even a corporal's chevron between them. "Or what, shit-for-brains? You and your mate want to make a fight of it?"

Burke looked at the group and he knew William was making exactly the same assessment as him. Johnny had five friends to back him up. One – the one who had called them out – was a natural leader. One was clearly hanging back, joining in the shouting only just enough to be accepted as one of the lads. Take out the leader quickly and that would leave Johnny and four of his mates, which seemed perfectly acceptable odds.

"Best you walk away." Burke spoke quietly but the air of menace caused the leader of the rabble to pause for a moment. Only a moment, though, before he took up the challenge. He reached toward the girl and ripped open her blouse.

Burke and William were close by now. Two quick steps brought Burke near enough for the leader to turn to watch him, preparing to fight. Johnny's attention was divided between his friend and the girl. He assumed, as did all the others, that Burke's first blow would be towards the leader. Instead, Burke reached out and grab the back of Johnny's collar. Moving fast now, he jerked his arm forward and Johnny's head smashed into the face of his friend. There was the sound of breaking cartilage and both men screamed as they went down. There was, it seemed to Burke, a quite unreasonable amount of blood.

To his left he could hear the sound of William's fist making a satisfying contact with somebody's gut, but he concentrated on the man in front of him who stood poised between attack and flight. The fellow's indecision was palpable and the result was all-too-predictable. Burke's left fist was smashing into his face as his right hit his solar plexus before he had even got his fists up to protect himself.

The others did not wait to share the same fate. Their boots clattered on the cobbles as they made a noisy and ignominious retreat.

James glanced across at William who was hauling his own victim back to his feet. "Too easy, really," he grumbled. "I was looking forward to a proper fight." As he spoke, he was taking off the man's jacket. He tossed it to James who stepped across to the girl who was pulling her tattered clothes around her.

"Put this on," he said.

The man whose jacket was being given away started to protest. That was a mistake. William held him firmly by one arm and with his free hand slapped him once on each cheek – palm of the hand first and back of the hand on the other side. "Piss off home, kid, and count yourself lucky to have got off so lightly."

The girl was still sitting on the stool she had used while sketching. She was pale but remarkably composed, given what had happened.

Burke helped her to her feet. "Can we take you home?"

She nodded and then gestured towards Johnny and his friend who were sitting up, groaning with their hands to their damaged faces. "What about them?" she said.

"What would you like?"

The girl did not reply but stepped over to where they were still sat on the ground. Many of the women in the area went barefoot, but she had small, but sturdy, shoes. Drawing her foot back she kicked very hard into Johnny's groin. He rolled back onto the ground and began to vomit.

The other man started to scrabble to his feet but a shove from William had him back on the ground. Before he could protect himself, the girl had handed out the same rough justice as she had on Johnny.

"Now we go home," she said. And, to William, "Can you carry my easel and paper?"

* * *

Home was a few hundred yards away, down one street, along an alley and then up a tiny cul-de-sac that Burke suspected he might well have passed on a dark night without even realising it was there.

Her house, sandwiched between its neighbours, was tiny but when she invited them in Burke saw it was immaculately clean and tidy. Her mother was there, which was as Burke had expected. How could a nice Catholic girl have invited them in otherwise?

Mother was a plump woman with a kindly face who could have been aged anything from thirty to sixty. At the sight of her daughter she rushed over demanding to know what had happened, desperate to reassure, even as she complained that her daughter had been plying her trade alone and that she should have stayed safe at home.

Looking past her daughter at the two soldiers escorting her, she prepared to launch an assault on them, blaming them – not unnaturally, it seemed to Burke – for the condition the girl was in. The girl hastened to explain what had happened and the next Burke knew they were being sat down and offered wine while her daughter – who had finally been properly introduced as Marta Cravinho – changed into a new blouse and rushed out to buy pastries.

Senhora Cravinho fussed about the dangers of her daughter's work. The girl had a natural talent as a artist and had found it a useful way to earn money once the soldiers came. "She got a few reais from neighbours who liked her pictures, but when the French came she realised that she could make real money selling pictures to their soldiers. Now she does it for the English. It's hardly any money to them, but it makes a huge difference to us. It's hard for two women living alone. But this isn't the first time she has been insulted – although there has never been anything as bad as this before. I think she will have to give it up and get work as …" She tailed off. Burke suspected that realistically there weren't all that many possibilities that didn't carry as many risks to her virtue as what she was doing now. She was a pretty girl – tall, slim, dark-haired and with a figure that

Burke had struggled to avoid looking at as he covered her with the purloined jacket. He had to agree, though, that she couldn't go back to sketching English soldiers – at least not until Johnny and his friends had left town. She had made dangerous enemies and the story would spread throughout the ranks. If she was seen out and about, she could well end up dead.

When Senhorita Cravinho arrived back with the pastries, her mother wasted no time in forbidding her to do any more sketching.

When Burke took her mother's side, explaining the danger that she was now in, she reluctantly accepted that her little business was at an end, but she was visibly distressed. The pastries were delicious, but the atmosphere meant that nobody seemed to be enjoying them much. Burke was worried that Marta might burst into tears at any moment.

"If it is so dangerous," said her mother, "perhaps she should stay at home for a while."

"I don't think you need to go that far." Burke did his best to sound reassuring. "Word will spread but they will know only that Johnny was humiliated by the girl who used to do the sketches. They won't know exactly what you look like."

And it was then that he realised how Marta could help with his own problem. He turned to her mother. He was going to need Senhora Cravinho's support if this idea was going to come to anything. "Actually," he said, "Marta might be able to help with a problem I have." Senhora Cravinho's expression suggested immediate scepticism. "There'd be money in it for her – good money."

At this, Marta interrupted before her mother could respond. "How much money? What do I have to do?"

"How much do you get paid for your sketches?"

"A few hundred reais. It depends on the sitter. If it is an officer I might even get five hundred reais."

"Could you sketch someone who wasn't sitting still for you? Someone drinking in a bar, for example."

She looked thoughtful. "Probably, yes. I can try anyway."

"I need some sketches. I will pay you an escudo for each one."

There was a sharp intake of breath from the mother. "What are you talking about? What do you really want? Nobody will pay an escudo for a drawing."

An escudo was over 1,500 reais. Burke realised that he should, perhaps not have offered so much, but he needed it to be enough to persuade Marta to join in a potentially dangerous adventure. And, while Senhora Cravinho was clearly suspicious, Marta was concentrating on the idea of earning more money than she had seen for a while. "When do you want this?"

"Next Tuesday."

"So long as that. Can't we start sooner."

"No. Next Tuesday. In a bar – *A Tendinha.* I want you to sketch some of the men there. If the people we are looking for do not turn up next Tuesday, I'll pay you – well, what do you think seems fair?"

Senhora Cravinho was having none of this. "You are paying my daughter to go with you to a bar! What sort of a girl do you think she is? You are no better than the other soldiers."

"Senhora, I am a British officer and you have my word that she will not be insulted. I will be sure to protect her."

"Pah! You are no officer. Look at your filthy coat. What kind of an idiot do you take me for?"

"No, mother!" Marta saw her commission vanishing away and she broke in. "You did not hear him when he spoke to the soldiers. He sounded like an officer."

"He is an officer, senhora," William joined in.

"So why does he not dress as an officer?"

That, Burke thought, was an excellent question. And it wasn't as if he could give an honest answer – we are spies in disguise looking for Portuguese traitors. Fortunately, William's imagination was quicker to come up with an explanation than his.

"We are on a special mission to find men like those who insulted your daughter and put an end to such behaviour. Obviously we cannot hope to succeed if we are dressed as officers."

"So you are like the secret police?"

It wasn't a comparison that particularly appealed to Burke, but it would do at a pinch. "A bit like secret police, senhora."

"And the men in the bar?"

"More secret work, senhora. But valuable and assisting your nation."

Marta was struggling to stay seated, so excited she had become. "It is valuable work and for our country," she said. "They don't even have to pay me if the men are not there. I just want to do this."

Poor girl! Burke thought. She was young – eighteen or nineteen, Burke guessed – and she probably imagined spying was exciting and romantic. Well, a couple of nights bored out of her wits in *A Tendinha* should disabuse her of those notions. Or perhaps not. She had probably led a sheltered life. She might think *A Tendinha* was exciting and romantic.

Her mother was still clearly uncomfortable but Burke could tell that her daughter's enthusiasm – and the money – was beginning to win her over. "And she'll be safe?"

"Absolutely." That was a lie. She'd probably be safe. "Sgt Brown and myself will be with her to look after her." That, at least, was true. He could only hope that nothing would go wrong.

CHAPTER 8: Back to 'A Tendinha'

They agreed to call on her the following Tuesday. Burke left money for clothes to replace the ones that had been torn. Senhora Cravinho at first refused to take it but Burke insisted. "It's the least I can do, senhora, to apologise for the vile behaviour of my countrymen. Besides, it's important that your daughter is wearing good clothes when we take her to *A Tendinha*. Respectable clothing will be the armour of her virtue."

That was an argument no decent Catholic mother could resist. Burke handed her some coins and he and William left with mother and daughter both promising undying friendship.

"Now," Burke said to William as they walked away, "we wait."

And waiting was all that Burke could do. He could not smarten his appearance. In fact, the enforced inactivity gave him more time to develop the badly shaven face and filthy hair of his new persona. It meant no socialising with the Portuguese aristocracy or even other British officers. He did venture out to Alfama a couple of times and he began to think he could find his way around the place in the dark. He also made a trip to Fletcher's headquarters and lurked in a doorway keeping watch on the place. He had no interest in who came and went – he only wanted to know how reliable the engineer's security arrangements were. After half an hour or so, Fletcher himself came out of the house and crossed to his doorway.

"Keeping an eye on us, I see."

At least, Burke thought, he didn't have to worry about carelessness there.

Most of the time he stayed in his room. Snr Lopez, he knew, would be too polite to comment on his appearance but it seemed easier to stay out of his way and avoid embarrassment. He tried to pass the time with Sousa's *Historia Genealogica da Casa Real Portugueza* on the grounds that understanding the history of the Portuguese royal family might give him some insight into the country's convoluted politics, but its twelve volumes defeated him and he was reduced to re-reading Frederick the Great's *History of the Seven Years' War*. He might have been deprived of a conventional military career, but he saw no reason why he should not be as well educated in military strategy as any more conventional officer.

There were letters from Beresford's office asking why he was absent from his post. The general had apparently found himself forced to spend time talking to petitioners himself and seemed unhappy with the situation. Burke sent a short reply saying that he was engaged on urgent business for Colonel Gordon. He imagined how much this would irritate Beresford and took some satisfaction in that.

Despite the time spent reading and baiting the general, the days dragged until the following Tuesday.

James and William set off to collect Marta at ten. Her mother fussed but there were no last-minute panics. She seemed reconciled to her daughter's enterprise and trusted to the two soldiers to bring her safely home.

William carried her paper – smaller sheets that she could work with at a table. She had no easel. "You'll sit with us," Burke explained, "and sketch me. If the men we are looking for arrive, change the paper and carry on sketching, but draw the man we point out to you. Try not to look directly at him. We'll move around if we have to, so you can see him over my shoulder."

She nodded. She seemed suddenly aware of the reality of what she was doing and Burke could sense her nerves.

"You'll be fine," he said. "We'll be there next to you all evening."

She gave a grateful smile and then they were at *A Tendinha* and making their way to the table where they had sat before. Burke sat with his back to the room, Marta opposite him with a good view of the customers with William beside her. There was no drawing for a while. They sat together, two soldiers and a pretty girl enjoying an evening's drinking. Despite her respectable clothing, Burke was sure that most people there would assume she was little better than a whore, but he hoped that none would know her well enough to recognise her in her usual surroundings.

Eventually William passed her a sheet of paper and she started to draw. There was a candle on the table and she moved it. "I want some light on your face, so I can see it to draw you."

"What about the other people here. It's all shadows and gloom. Will you be able to draw them?"

"I can try."

She took up her pencil and began to sketch. Burke sat still in half-profile. He had held the pose for several minutes when he realised that she was not looking at him but at someone over his shoulder. Her pencil was moving quickly and hardly had he realised what she was doing than she passed him the sheet.

It was a sketch and not the finished drawing she would have produced for a paying customer who had sat still for her in a good light. But the face in the sketch was vivid and, as he saw when he glanced over his shoulder, easily recognisable as one of the men playing dominoes at a table behind him.

He smiled his appreciation and the three of them sat for a while, sipping at their wine. More accurately, Marta sipped at her wine while Burke and William made more serious inroads into theirs. More wine arrived. (The waitress recognised Burke from his previous visit and obviously remembered his tip.) Marta took one more sip and started sketching again. This time she looked directly at Burke, taking her time with the drawing.

Burke was again sitting with his back to the room while William could see the picture taking shape. He was clearly impressed. In fact, he was so caught up with it that he almost missed the arrival of Morais and Carvalho. Fortunately, the fuss surrounding their arrival, as less prestigious customers gave up their seats, caught his eye. "They're here," he said.

Burke did not move. "Keep sketching, senhorita," he said.

Marta smiled. "If you are trying to remain inconspicuous, you had best call me Marta. Nobody here is calling their companions 'senhorita'."

"A good point. But I think we'll go with Margarida. And I am David. It's safer."

"Might we be in danger?"

"Not if we are careful. Two have just arrived. Bob – for I've this minute rechristened him – will point them out to you if you don't recognise them. They will stand out because of their fine clothes." Marta's head started to move. "Don't turn your head. Glance from the corner of your eyes. It's important they don't know they are being watched."

Burke could see the girl's hand hesitate as she sketched. "Are these the men you want me to draw?"

"No. We expect them to be joined by others. Those are the ones we want you to draw. Until then, just carry on with me."

She bent to the pad but Burke noticed her starting to bite her lip. It was as if she had only now realised the situation she had found herself in.

"Relax, Margarida. Take a break from drawing for a minute and have some more of your wine. You've barely touched it."

"I need a steady hand to draw."

"Your hand isn't steady now. You're too tense. Take a sip of wine and relax."

She raised her glass to her lips and took a tiny sip.

Burke caught William's eye and his sergeant took up the conversational challenge.

"Did I ever tell you about the colonel I had before I was working for David here?"

James and Marta both shook their heads, though James was pretty sure he had already heard the anecdote William was about to offer. It was a good story and might well lift the mood.

"He was a fearsome man and everyone went in dread of him, but there was one young lieutenant who was desperate for leave. He said his mother was sick, but we all knew he was after seeing his sweetheart who he had heard was setting her cap at another man. Anyway, he approaches the colonel and asks for six days' leave. The colonel, who was in a moody humour, answered, "Go to hell!" The lieutenant paused for a moment and then asked, "Has your honour any orders for the devil?" There were several seconds of terrible silence and then the colonel burst into laughter, doubled the man's leave and gave him a pound towards the expenses of his journey."

Burke was relieved to see Marta laugh and take another, longer, drink from her glass. Her attack of nerves seemed to have passed and the three of them chatted easily for a while before William turned to her and suggested she should take up a new sheet of paper.

"Why would I? I haven't finished this one yet." And, suddenly realising what he meant: "They're here, aren't they?"

"Only one of them. He's moving over to them now, so there's no hurry. And there's nothing to worry about. You've been here sketching for a while, having a drink, sharing a laugh. You're part of the scenery now."

Burke saw her eyes move to where he knew Morais and Carvalho were sitting. For a moment he saw the flicker of alarm in her eyes and then she started to sketch. As she drew, he could see her relaxing, caught up in her task, her eyes flicking up only as she needed to concentrate on details of the face she was drawing.

Several minutes passed. Burke watched the girl anxiously. Based on the previous week, she only had a few minutes to finish.

Suddenly she took a fresh sheet of paper and, putting it over the one she had been working on, she started afresh.

"You don't have time to start over." Burke spoke quietly but urgently. "Do the best you can with what you've got."

The girl lifted her eyes from the paper and smiled. "The first one's finished but it's in profile. By now I've caught enough glimpses of his face to be able to give you an idea of what he looks like straight on." She glanced over Burke's shoulder and her hand moved even faster. "I think he's getting ready to leave."

She was totally absorbed in her drawing now as William gave James a running commentary on what was happening behind him. "Morais is reaching across to the bloke. I don't see money passing – there are shadows and he was quick. The bloke's nodding though. And now he's getting up."

Marta carried on sketching, even as her unwitting sitter left.

"It's alright, Margarida." Burke's tone was reassuring. "You did your best, but he's gone."

"Be quiet." Marta's tone was sharp. "I'm concentrating."

Across the table, William could see the sketch though James could not. He gave Burke a brief nod of reassurance.

Marta's pencil slowed and finally stopped. A couple more lines, a little shading and she handed both sheets to Burke.

He held them up so he could see them in the candlelight. He sat silently, looking at them and saying nothing. Then, to Marta, "I seem to owe you two escudos."

* * *

The second man arrived soon after and the whole exercise was repeated. This time Marta was able to catch him in half-profile and there was only one sketch, but Burke was happy that you could identify the man from his picture.

Morais and Carvalho left soon after. It seemed there would be no third man tonight.

Burke ordered more wine and this time Marta was more than happy to join the drinking. It was a happy trio that left *A Tendinha* half an hour later.

James and William saw Marta back to her door. It was common courtesy but, in any case, they would never have left a young woman to make her way through Alfama at night. Her mother was awake and scolded them for being so late, but James had come prepared with money and the sight of the three gold escudos being pressed into Marta's hand led to their immediate forgiveness.

"There's another 500 reais if you can draw two good copies of each of these. I'm nervous that all your work will be for nothing if we lose the drawings."

"What are you going to do with them?"

"We're going to show them to some people we know." He smiled. "Your work will be quite famous." And then, more seriously: "Though it's probably best that the artist remains anonymous."

* * *

The next morning William shaved Burke and recovered a fashionable cut from beneath the shaggy mass of hair that he had sported for over a week. Burke stood before a mirror and looked appreciatively at the results. "Thank God for that," he told William. "I had feared I would have to take to wearing a wig." Burke had never worn a wig, considering them ridiculously old-fashioned. He supposed that, if William's efforts had been totally unacceptable, he might have been driven to such a desperate resort, but Sgt Brown had, as ever, saved the day. By the time he had his uniform on, he felt ready to face the world again.

At breakfast he apologised to Snr Lopez, claiming that he had been avoiding his host as he had been unwell. It was not an entirely convincing story but it allowed both men to resume normal life as if nothing strange had happened.

Burke dawdled over breakfast, giving William time to return from his visit to Marta. He returned just as Burke started his fourth cup of coffee. He placed the original sketches and the copies on the breakfast table. Burke looked from one to the other and could not tell them apart.

"She's good, isn't she?" said William. "I reckon she must have been up since the crack of dawn to get those done."

Burke had his doubts, given how fast she could draw, but however long she had spent on them, the quality was remarkable.

"I must start getting these shown around. Starting, I think, with Colonel Fletcher."

CHAPTER 9: The Lines of Torres Vedras

By noon he was in Fletcher's office, showing him the pictures.

Fletcher looked at them carefully before shaking his head. "I haven't seen them around here – or anywhere else for that matter. I can show them round the staff if you like."

Burke did like, and he followed Fletcher as he moved from room to room, passing the pictures around the men working there. There were drawing rooms, with men working at chart tables; offices where clerks placed orders for food and transport; a map room, where Fletcher was drawn into a heated debate about whether an additional fort was required to cover an almost imperceptible gap in the wall of artillery that would soon protect Lisbon. Burke was fascinated by the scale of the enterprise and the industry of the men carrying it out, but there was nobody who admitted to seeing either of the two possible spies.

Back in his office, Fletcher looked again at the pictures and asked Burke where he had got them. "In a tavern," he said, careful not to give any details pointing back to Morais and Carvalho. Fletcher was not the only one to take security seriously.

"They look quite a rough sort of fellow. What kind of a tavern was it?"

"A rough sort of tavern would be a fair description."

Fletcher gestured at the pictures. "Anyone looking like that would stand out if they spent long hanging around in this area. Look at how quickly you were noticed."

Burke nodded. "I had to ask, though. I've good reason to think that they are passing on some sort of information and this, as you've pointed out, is the most valuable information they could obtain."

Fletcher nodded in his turn. "The secret of the lines of Torres Vedras. Yes, it's certainly the most valuable secret we have, but our offices here aren't the only way of penetrating it." Burke raised an interrogative eyebrow. "Spies could always just go to see the lines for themselves."

"Would that be possible?"

"It's not impossible, though it wouldn't be straightforward. The men who are working on the Lines only see the forts they are working on, so they have no idea of the extent of the work. And we keep them there: they don't get to return regularly to Lisbon, so rumours don't spread."

"But some people go and come?"

"Yes. The men who take up the provisions have to drive up and back. They don't see much but if they make enough trips they may start to put a picture together."

Fletcher, it turned out, did not employ the drivers directly. As with much of the labour force working on the Lines, he used civilian workers. Provisioning was contracted out to several different suppliers. "That way nobody gets to see the scale of the thing." It did mean, though, that drivers came from many different firm and that Fletcher had no way of knowing who they were.

The logic of the situation was obvious to both of them. Somebody needed to ride out to the Lines and show the drawings to people there.

"It's out of the question to show them to everybody. It would take far too long. But at the moment we're working in half a dozen areas and each section is supplied by the same merchant. We could make a start by checking a couple of the districts ourselves."

"How long will it take to travel from one district to another? That looks like very rough country."

Fletcher, who had been looking increasingly unhappy at the idea that his security might be breached, now relaxed into his habitual grin.

"Not as rough as you might think."

He moved to the table, with its usual collection of plans and sketches, and unrolled a map of the whole area covered by the works.

"The idea behind the Lines is that they follow the line of the countryside. Basically they all lie along this ridge here." Fletcher's finger traced a route along the top of the hills that separated Lisbon from the plains to the north.

"And these forts here?" Burke pointed at another line of fortifications further south.

"That's a second line of defence in the unlikely events that the French breach the first line." Then, in response to Burke's sceptical expression. "You know Wellington. He always likes to have a firm position to fall back on."

It was true, Burke knew. Wellington had an excellent eye for the lie of the land. His understanding of the terrain where he would be fighting was reinforced by the time he spent fox-hunting. His fox-hunts were famous for never catching any foxes (his hounds were in a terrible state after years of following the army) but the hours he spent in the saddle were invaluable when it came to planning the way to use the ground to favour the British Army at the expense of the French – and he never relied on having only one possible place to position his forces if he could identify two. Even so, the idea of building one line of fortifications across 30 miles of rough country was ambitious enough. Only Wellington, Burke thought, could have suggested that there should be further fortifications, just in case.

Fletcher pointed out more detail on the map. The Lines did not simply consist of fortifications – some full-scale forts, others more simple gun positions. Wellington had also ordered the building of a military road running behind the lines, connecting all the positions. "It's a properly stone surfaced road that you can move on quickly. It means that we can leave the forts manned by local militia and have regular British units positioned behind the lines so that they can be moved rapidly to anywhere that needs our trained troops to defend it. And it's invaluable for bringing up supplies or just moving from position to position when I'm carrying out an inspection. Which I rather think I'm going to do in the next couple of days. Would you like to come?"

Of course he'd like to come. He didn't want to hand over the copies of Marta's work. They were too important to risk losing. But even if he hadn't thought that a trip to the Lines was the best way to push his mission forward, he would still have wanted to see them. Looking at them on a map they seemed impressive enough but he wanted to see this astonishing project of military engineering for himself.

It was soon enough arranged. Fletcher was not a man to waste time once he had decided what needed to be done.

They rode north the next day: Burke, Fletcher and Major Batarda from the Portuguese militia. Burke had suggested bringing William but Fletcher had objected. "I have to be there," he said, "and you have to be there. Major Batarda is coming because we rely entirely on the efforts of the Portuguese militia and it's important that they see themselves as valued members of our enterprise. Too many in the Army view the Portuguese as somehow junior partners in our alliance. It rankles with the Portuguese. It is their country and their people who bear the heaviest load in this war. I am careful to make every effort to recognise their role." William, he suggested politely but firmly, had no business on their trip.

Burke had to acknowledge that Fletcher had a point. William could remain in Lisbon and continue to ferret for any scraps of gossip that might sharpen the picture of the alliances and rivalries within the Portuguese aristocracy. In the end, Burke thought, such knowledge could be crucial. It seemed to him that any decision made by these people to betray their country was less because of a commitment to France or an ideological belief in revolution and more as part of some settling of ancient scores. The city dwellers looked down on the rural aristocracy while the landed counts and viscounts sneered at the men in Lisbon. The ancient families had nothing but contempt for those ennobled more recently and the newcomers saw the older families as out of touch and holding the country back. Then there were feuds that went back hundreds of years to when somebody's great-great-great grandfather had insulted somebody's great-great-great grandmother's sister and the families still refused to acknowledge each other today. In Portugal, it seemed, the political was very, very personal. He would leave William behind and hope that his sergeant came up with something useful.

For now, though, he would enjoy the ride in the open air, leaving behind the stench of the city and its sordid world of scandals and spite. It was approaching high summer. The sun was blazing and it was hot for riding but he was in good company – Major Batarda seemed to share Fletcher's cheerful attitude to life – and they made their way easily across level fields and through small villages of whitewashed buildings which showed few signs of the ravages of armed conflict.

After a while the country grew rougher and they seemed to spend most of their time pushing uphill, but the terrain was far from mountainous. There were fewer villages but the land was dotted with conical white windmills and had a generally peaceful and prosperous air. They were hundreds of miles from any French armies and they saw no soldiers as they rode. It was easy to forget for a while that they were at war.

Burke's first sight of the Lines was an anti-climax. He hardly saw the redoubt, which seemed to flow naturally out of the countryside.

"That's because we build them on the ridge-line so they fit with the contours. And they are earthworks rather than stone structures, so they can be easily missed coming from the south. They look a bit different from the other side of the ridge."

Fletcher pushed his horse past the redoubt and Burke followed until he could see the ground falling away to the north. Here the evidence of the efforts of Fletcher's men was immediately obvious.

The southern slope of the ridge was wooded. It was hardly a great forest, but the land was too steep for cultivation and trees had grown up, providing some pleasant greenery and shade on a hot day. The northern slope, though, was bare. Hundreds of stumps showed where trees had grown but they had all been cut down.

"It gives us a clear field of fire," said Fletcher.

Burke looked down the slope. It wasn't that steep, but troops attacking the redoubt would be slowed as they toiled up under their packs and they would be under fire the whole time. At the top the earthworks had been created from soil dug from the ground so that first the French would have to clamber into a ditch at the foot of the redoubt's wall, which would be around twenty feet above them. "Poor buggers," he thought. "They won't stand a chance."

Six cannon covered any possible approach from the north with slit trenches running out from the fort to allow troops to cover its flanks. It was an imposing position but Burke saw only a few militia troops lounging around the position.

"How many men does it need to hold it?"

"It's barely finished so it's not properly manned yet. Once we're ready to meet the French there'll be 300 men garrisoned here."

"Our men?"

"Maybe a few here and there, but we're basically relying on the militia. If they are attacked, it will take a while for the French to overwhelm them, even if half of the fellows run away. And before that time, we'll have British reinforcements up to do the business. Come on, I'll show you the road."

They dropped back down to the south. The only road Burke had noticed as they rode to the fort was an old cart track. It was wide enough, he supposed, and firm underfoot, but hardly the military road that Fletcher had promised.

"Is the road not finished here?"

"It doesn't need to be. This track does all we need. Where it doesn't, we've repaired it with stone. There's no point in building a new road when there's a perfectly good old one here already."

They followed the track westward for a mile or so. Here and there, Burke saw the repairs Fletcher had spoken about. He'd been on better roads, but it did seem this one was adequate to the task. They emerged from a small wood (no clearance of timber this side of the lines) to see the track drop away to their left. Ahead, though, was what was clearly a new road, wide and straight.

"It's beaten earth for now," said Fletcher, "but we'll have proper stone paving in place by winter."

They passed other small forts as they rode on. Some were still being built. At one, Burke saw a couple of officers in the uniform of the Engineers and Fletcher stopped to chat to them for a few minutes. It gave Burke a chance to see the mechanics of building the defences. There were three lines of workmen – Portuguese civilians from the look of them. One line was digging out a ditch and the other two piling up the spoil into ramparts and parapets. At one point where the parapet had apparently reached its final height, other workmen were hammering it flat into a solid mass.

Major Batarda watched Burke watching the workmen, a smile on his lips. "It's an impressive sight, is it not?"

Burke had to agree that it was. "But why is it only here that I see our Engineering officers? Who is supervising the work in the other forts?"

"You are one of those Englishmen who believe that the Portuguese can do nothing without your countrymen overseeing them?" The smile that still hovered about his lips suggested he was more amused than angry. "Colonel Fletcher has more faith in us. There will be a couple of Engineering officers when work starts. They will mark out where the digging is to take place and stay a few days to make sure there are no unexpected problems. After that, it is left to us to get on with it." He looked at the three lines of sweating men. "I think we do quite a good job, no?"

"A remarkable effort. How do you maintain discipline?"

"You mean how to we get the men to work without whipping them like you do in your army?" Burke gave an embarrassed shrug. He was not proud of the British enthusiasm for corporal punishment – he had known of a man given 300 lashes for a dirty button – but it was the way it was and it did seem to work. "We pay them, Senhor Burke. And we pay them well."

"Lucky you," thought Burke. The British troops in Spain were always being promised their arrears of pay but the supply of money from London was, at best, intermittent and most of what there was had already been spoken for. Too many of the merchants Wellington relied on to feed his army were impatient to be paid themselves.

"Besides," Batarda continued, "we have an advantage over your English soldiers. We are fighting in our own country against an enemy who has invaded us. They've pillaged our lands, burned down our houses, insulted our womenfolk. When you have faced all that, you do not need to be whipped to fight the French."

"But you know why I am here."

"Hunting a traitor. I know. And when you find him, I hope you kill him. But the man in your picture – the man who looks like one of these workmen – he doesn't know how to get a message to the French. I don't know how you found him, but my guess is that you saw him talking to someone who might know how to contact the enemy."

Burke's success at cards owed something to his ability to present an unreadable face to the world, but there must have been some flicker of response to Batarda's comment because the major smiled again. "An aristocrat, I suspect. Someone who has no real sympathy for the working men of this country, someone who is more concerned about his position and his future than that of the people who toil in his fields or sail the ships that bring his goods from Brazil and China and Africa. You need to look there for your traitors, colonel. It is the rich that will betray their country, not the poor."

Fletcher had finished his conversation and arrived just in time to overhear Batarda's final comments.

"I see the major has been making you nervous with his radical views. Don't worry, Burke. His rhetoric may be revolutionary but he's a fine engineer and committed to the defeat of the French."

Batarda smiled again: his good humour seemed inexhaustible. "Colonel Fletcher is right, of course. Nothing else can be as important as the defeat of the French. And the Emperor Napoleon is perhaps the greatest of all the aristos. After all, the ruler of the French used only to be a king. But after they cut off their king's head, they replaced him with an emperor. But perhaps the Portuguese might adopt some of the less bloodthirsty ideas of the French to make life better for the common man here."

"It's a good thing you are among friends here, major. The excesses of Pombal's years may be behind you, but that doesn't mean that talk like that can't get you into trouble."

Burke had heard of Pombal. "I thought he would have appealed to you, major. Wasn't he against the power of the church and in favour of reform?"

For once, Batarda did not smile. "He achieved a lot. He was responsible for the rebuilding of Lisbon after the earthquake. But he did not tolerate dissent. If you were heard disagreeing with his policies, you vanished. It was not a good time."

"But he's gone now." Fletcher was determined to get the conversation onto safer ground. "Now we can concentrate on beating the French."

"Except that there seem to be those fighting their own war, where the French are not, perhaps, the enemy. Isn't that why you are here, Colonel Burke?"

Burke developed a sudden interest in the condition of the road ahead, pulling his horse to one side to avoid an area where the surface had broken up. When he spoke, his voice was carefully neutral. "We don't really know what is going on. We do think that the men in the pictures are selling information. It may be that they are spying on someone's wife or someone's mistress and that it is no concern of anyone except their husbands or lovers. It may be that they are informers, doing their civic duty in reporting criminals and being rewarded for it. But there is something that seems not quite right about what we have seen and we have to consider the possibility that they are selling military secrets. In any case, we'd like a word with them."

"And you think you will find them here?"

"It's a possibility."

Now all three men concentrated on the road, although it was no worse than it had been when they first joined it. The weather remained fine and the countryside green and fertile, but somehow their good spirits had evaporated and they rode the next few miles in silence.

* * *

The first they saw of the Great Redoubt was what looked like a mast, apparently situated on the peak of one of the hills, reaching far into the sky. In fact, Burke had caught glimpses of it at several points during their ride, but had dismissed it as some random folly or a mark for the Engineers' surveying apparatus. Close too, though, it seemed like something transplanted from a ship. Towards the top of the mast was a spar that stuck out from it at right angles. Unlike the arrangement in a ship, the spar was almost entirely on one side of the mast and there were no sails although, now that they were closer, Burke could see what looked like rigging running from the spar to the ground.

Fletcher noticed the puzzled look on Burke's face. "It's a telegraph. Naval idea – but these sailors can be pretty smart when they put their minds to it. When it's working there will be an arrangement of balls hanging from the spars and we can use it to pass messages along the Lines. A bit like the signal flags on a ship, but easier to read on a still day. We're going to have some ratings lent to us to show us how it's done. There's nothing to see yet, though. We're still finishing off here. It's quite a big place."

Burke could see that. Although they were approaching from the south, there were embrasures bristling with cannon to cover the gate against a French attack. Almost automatically he started to count them.

"There are thirteen," Fletcher said helpfully. "And one tucked around the corner covering the secondary gate. We have another fourteen on the other side to fire on the French as they approach from the north. That's the main business of the fort, of course, but this one is our headquarters for this section of the Lines. It means we have a larger garrison and have to make more provision than usual for defence."

Burke was impressed. The fort was far from regular, so he couldn't see from one end of the walls to the other, making it difficult to judge its size but he thought it was probably almost 200 yards, running roughly west to east.

"How many men in this garrison?"

"There'll be 1,590 men and 27 guns. That gives some idea of the scale of the undertaking. Around half of the garrison are already here, getting the guns into position, providing some covering force for neighbouring forts, helping with the last of the building and so on."

They were riding through the entrance now: solid double gates open, but guards ready to close them at the first sign of trouble. Inside, Burke saw activity everywhere. Cannon were being manhandled onto gun platforms, masons were working on a substantial stone building, while workmen carried planks of wood down ramps that disappeared into underground storage. Again Fletcher noticed Burke's interest and explained.

"We store powder underground. We don't want a lucky French shell to blow up our ammunition store. The walls and roof are stone but we need to protect the powder from the damp. The base is beaten earth so we put in an air gap and lay down a wooden floor above that."

Now the mounds of earth dotted apparently randomly around the interior of the fort made sense: they provided avenues of shelter for soldiers carrying ammunition from the stores to the cannon. More earthworks showed where there were smaller forts inside the main wall. If the French breached the outer defences it was clear that the defenders intended to fall back into these enclaves and do their best to hold out until reinforcements arrived.

"We've got this place already part-garrisoned because it's being used as an administrative centre. For example, supplies arrive here and are distributed to other forts." Fletcher looked across the compound to where a couple of waggons were being unloaded. "It looks like we're in luck. The supplies are here now and we can enquire about your mysterious spy."

Burke was not fooled for a moment. Fletcher was not a man who would ever leave anything to luck. He had obviously known when the supplies were due and timed their arrival accordingly. Still, he went along with the charade and the three of them walked their horses toward the wagons as if this were a casual visit.

As they crossed the fort an Engineer officer who had been supervising the placement of the cannon noticed his colonel and hurried across to meet them, snapping a crisp salute as he arrived.

"Good afternoon, colonel." He stood to attention waiting to see what had brought his colonel to the redoubt.

"At ease, Tyler. All's well. Fact is we're looking for a civilian chap we'd like a word with. You haven't seen this fellow around, have you?"

Burke produced the picture and handed it to Tyler.

"Difficult to say, really. It could be anyone. It looks a bit like one of the men who came up with today's supplies. Him over there." He nodded over to where the wagons were being unloaded.

The three of them dismounted. "I think we'll saunter over and have a word," said Fletcher. "Nothing for you to worry about, Tyler. You get back to your cannon."

They walked on, leading their horses. Burke thought Fletcher was handling it rather well. 'Softly, softly catchee monkey,' was generally the best way to proceed.

Whether it was that the man had noticed Tyler's nod or was just panicked by the sight of three red coated officers moving towards him, 'softly, softly' turned out to be unlikely to catch anyone that day. The man dropped the barrel he was carrying and took off at a run.

Batarda and Burke took off after him while Fletcher remounted and turned his horse in the direction the man was heading.

Batarda was soon ahead of Burke and closing fast on their prey. Burke, breathing hard, fell back. Sometimes he felt he was getting too old for this work.

The fugitive swerved to avoid a party of militia drilling nearby and Batarda gained another couple of yards on him.

Burke admitted later that the militia man had only been trying to help. There was someone fleeing three officers. He was obviously a villain of some sort and the platoon had been practicing loading their muskets. It was the work of a moment to put priming powder in the pan.

A single shot rang out and the fugitive dropped.

Batarda, Burke and Fletcher gathered to look down at the body. There was a small hole in his back where the ball had entered and, when they turned him over, a much larger one in his chest where it had exited. It was probably the most accurate shot his killer had ever made.

"Damn," said Burke.

* * *

If anybody knew anything about the dead man, they weren't admitting it. The other men who had travelled up with him only knew him as Cristiano. He had joined the firm supplying the Grand Redoubt only recently. "He kept himself to himself," said one of them. "Bit of an odd bloke," said another. "Useless with the mules but a hard enough worker."

"I'll have a word with the people who hired him when we get back to Lisbon," said Burke. "But I doubt we'll find anything useful."

Fletcher agreed. "At least we know that there really is an attempt to spy on our work but if we're lucky we've scotched that snake."

"Hardly," said Burke. "We think there were at least three of them."

"Two you have pictures of and a third you haven't seen?"

"Oh we've seen him. We just don't have a picture."

Fletcher pursed his lips. "I'd intended just to come up here, mainly to reassure myself and you, but I think we need at least to travel to the fort at San Vicente."

"San Vicente?"

"It's the biggest of all the forts. It overlooks the town of Torres Vedras itself. It's another centre for distributing supplies. We should show the garrison commander your other picture and warn him to be on guard."

Burke agreed with his logic.

"It's a four-hour ride, though, and takes us further from Lisbon."

"Best we start out now," suggested Batarda.

Fletcher grimaced toward Burke. "The enthusiasm of youth. And no regard for old men's posteriors."

In the end, despite Batarda's eagerness, they decided to take a short break to eat before pushing on. "After all," said Fletcher, "I'd be remiss in my duty if I did not ensure that the supplies that have just arrived are as specified."

The carts had brought up beef, bread, pease, cheese and rice – the standard fare of the British Army, though Burke was none too pleased to see that the workmen in the forts were being fed better than the Army he had left behind in Spain whose rations arrived only intermittently. Fletcher sniffed the beef and announced that it would not kill anybody but it would need to be boiled for a while to make it edible. The three of them had little time to spend over their meal so in the end they settled for bread and cheese, washed down with some of the wine that replaced small beer as the beverage of choice for the Portuguese.

It was not the finest of meals but after a morning in the saddle they were all hungry and happy enough with local cheese eaten with bread that was not all that stale.

All too soon, though, or so it seemed to Burke, he had to swing himself back into the saddle and they were off again, following the road that connected the forts as it ran north westward. It had been a while since he had ridden such a distance and the aches he was already feeling suggested that he was going to be stiff and sore the next day.

For now, though, they were all refreshed after their break and they made good time along the military road. They pushed on past several more forts without stopping. Some, like the Grand Redoubt, were finished, or almost finished. Others were barely started and at one point they saw two Engineers with knotted ropes marking out the place where the ditch was to be dug while workmen stood ready to start as soon as the ropes were in place.

No two of the forts were identical. The uneven terrain meant that each fitted its surrounding as if an organic thing, growing from the earth. Some were small, hardly more than gun platforms protected by ditch and earth rampart, others were elaborate forts – smaller than the Grand Redoubt, but significant strong points with garrisons that could run to hundreds of men. Many were built around the conical whitewashed windmills of the region, looking forlorn stripped of their sails. Batarda explained to James that the windmills, being generally situated on the top of hills, were usually at convenient places to put forts and the solid buildings provided secure accommodation for ammunition.

Burke was used to the idea that normal life was destroyed as armies swept through a country but this was the first time he had seen the destruction of so many livelihoods by the army that was there to defend the people – and that before there was any sign of the enemy. And this, he knew, was nothing compared to what would happen north of the Lines, where Wellington's plan to starve the French into submission meant the destruction of farms, crops and livestock throughout the countryside and the evacuation of the people into Lisbon. He thought how crowded the city was already with so many troops passing through. The idea of it housing thousands more was terrifying.

There was nothing to be gained by dwelling on this. He decided instead to concentrate on the ride.

The countryside was beautiful. From the road they had wonderful views out to the south. They passed ancient olive groves and fields where cattle grazed alongside whitewashed farms, looking like children's toys in the distance. It was sunny and warm but not too hot – ideal riding weather.

Burke allowed his horse to dawdle behind Fletcher and after a while Batarda fell back to ride alongside him. The road was wide enough for them to ride comfortably side by side and Burke, looking for a safe subject for conversation, remarked on how impressed he was with the work of the Engineers.

"It's a good road," Batarda agreed, "but it's all in a day's work for the Engineers. An army can't travel without roads and in Spain many of the roads are barely better than tracks. We build roads all the time." He was dismissive of the effort and Burke concluded that Major Batarda had not been involved with this aspect of Fletcher's plans. "It's the Lines that inspire me. Colonel Fletcher's vision is remarkable. Not the individual forts, though many of them are feats of military building in themselves, but the way that they combine, each covering its neighbours and all presenting an impregnable barrier to attack from the north." He paused, aware, Burke thought, that he was letting his enthusiasm run away with him. "But you, colonel, what is your interest in the Lines? I know we came looking for a spy and it seems we found one. But what brought you here in the first place?"

"We received intelligence that the French might be active in gathering secret information in Lisbon. The Lines seemed to be an obvious target for their activities."

"You received intelligence." Batarda did not attempt to hide his amusement. "I enquired about you, colonel. Nobody seems to know exactly what you are doing in Lisbon."

Burke should have been annoyed, he knew, but it was difficult to resent Batarda's curiosity. That didn't mean that he was going to tell him the truth.

"I'm a liaison officer for General Beresford," he said. "I deal with relations between our army and the locals."

"And the locals warned you about French spies."

Burke was happy to agree with Batarda's suggestion.

"And General Beresford can spare you to come up here and investigate?" His amusement was again obvious.

"I had some leave. I thought it would be interesting to see the forts."

Unnoticed by the two of them, Fletcher had reined his horse in and had listened to the last exchange. "Stop teasing Colonel Burke," he said. "He's told you all he can."

After that the conversation stayed on carefully neutral topics: the scenery, the weather, the beauty of Portuguese women, and the relative merits of fish (championed by Batarda) and beef (favoured by Burke).

It was late in the afternoon before Fletcher pointed ahead. "Fort San Vicente," he said.

It was an impressive structure, much bigger than the Grand Redoubt. Much of it was faced with stone, making it look more like Burke's idea of a traditional fort. Its shape was so irregular, though, that he could get no idea of its size.

"It defends Torres Vedras itself." Batarda was clearly proud of what the Engineers had achieved here. "It's a key point of communication between the north and Lisbon, so it's the strongest of all the forts."

As they rode up to the main gate they passed under a battery of four cannon covering the steep path. Anyone attacking this place was going to take very heavy casualties.

Batarda was still boasting of the merits of the place. “Technically it’s three redoubts, two facing roughly north-east and a defensive redoubt facing south-west. The whole thing is joined by a large open space to shelter troops, with bomb-proof traverses so they can move safely to whichever redoubt needs reinforcing. Even if the French breached the walls – and I can hardly believe that would ever happen – the redoubts will hold out individually.”

They were through the gates and Burke could see for himself how big the central area was – about 200 yards long. They turned to the right and through another set of gates and, to his surprise, Burke saw a small church ahead of him.

“Used to be a hermitage,” said Fletcher. “I’m afraid we’ve kicked the hermit out. And, godless chaps that we are, we’re using the chapel as our headquarters here.”

As if on cue an Engineer emerged from the chapel and saluted.

“What brings you to our humble home, colonel.”

“Trouble, I’m afraid, Bryant.” Fletcher introduced Burke and explained the reason for their visit.

Major Bryant pored over the pictures – one full face and one in half-profile – and shook his head. “Doesn’t look like anyone I recognise. There are hardly any civilian workers here now. As you can see, we’re pretty well finished. I’m sure this isn’t one of the fellows here.”

“We think it’s most likely one of the men who drive up with supplies.”

“You’ve missed them, I’m afraid. We’re not expecting anything else for a week.”

There was, it seemed, nothing for it but to leave the pictures with Bryant, who promised to pass them around the militia officers in case any of them recognised him. “And next week I’ll make sure to check all the men on the supply waggons myself.”

It was a frustrating visit, but Burke was used to dead ends in his line of work but there was always a chance that Bryant would recognise someone the following week. “But if you do,” said Burke, “try to take him alive.”

CHAPTER 10: Fruitless visits to the grocers

The journey home passed without incident. They had stayed overnight at San Vicente and had been sent on their way well-fed and well-rested. They were back in Lisbon soon after noon and Burke sat down with William to plan his next steps.

"We know now that there really are spies poking around the Lines. We've seen three but we only have pictures of two. I think the first obvious thing to do is to try to get a picture of the third. We should spend some more time at *A Tendinha* to see if there are any more men keeping assignations with Morais and Carvalho – and by 'we' I mean you. I can't go round looking like a scarecrow for another fortnight. Apart from anything else I need to pay visits to all Colonel Fletcher's suppliers. Take Marta and get sketches of anyone we've missed."

William agreed enthusiastically. He liked Marta and welcomed the opportunity to see her again and offer her the chance to make more money. He was happy to leave Burke to the tedious business of checking all the suppliers – but not until he had dusted off his uniform. "You can't go out like that, sir. It's covered with dirt from the road."

Burke submitted to waiting until William was satisfied that he was fit to be seen in public and then set out to start his inquiries. He didn't want to delay. The events at the Grand Redoubt had convinced him that the danger of the secret of the Lines falling into French hands was real and urgent.

He started at the offices of Snr Solis, purveyor (according to the sign above his premises) of all sorts of comestibles. He had been the employer of the unfortunate individual who had died at the Grand Redoubt. Burke's detour via San Vicente meant that he arrived after news of the carrier's death had already reached Snr Solis, but business seems to be going on as usual. If anyone had been upset about Cristiano's death, they weren't showing it.

"He was new," Snr Solis explained. "Nobody really knew him."

"How did he get the job?"

Snr Solis grimaced. “That was a bit odd. He came in a few weeks ago and asked if there was any work and we said we had all the men we needed. A couple of days after that one of our workers was killed. They say it was a robbery, but I suspect it was a tavern brawl and people are just being kind. Anyway, the next day this Cristiano is back. Are there still no vacancies? And, of course, there was a vacancy then, so he got the job.”

“Any references?”

Solis gave a short bark of laughter. “It’s not that sort of job. You’re never out on your own, so you start with a more experienced man and if he doesn’t think you’re up to the work, you’re out and we hire someone else. Usually one of our fellows will recommend somebody but, as I said, Cristiano turned up at exactly the right time and we hadn’t had time to put the word out so…” He shrugged.

“Didn't you think it was odd, him turning up so conveniently?”

“It did seem strange, but it's hardly as if he would have killed somebody to get a job like this, is it?”

Burke nodded but said nothing. Was it possible? He rather feared it was.

* * *

He called on three more businesses that afternoon. It was clear that Fletcher had spread his net widely in his search for suppliers. The places Burke visited ranged from a glorified greengrocer with one battered cart for delivering vegetables, to a thriving enterprise which could supply meat, fish or vegetables and whose premises included warehouses and stabling for the horses that pulled their fleet of carts. The owner of this place had seemed nervous when Burke turned up, which he was prepared to view as suspicious. It turned out, though, that he was just worried that Burke might be there to complain. Recently, some of the wine he supplied had been so sour as to be undrinkable and a consignment of beef had been maggoty. He was full of apologies and insistent that he had no idea how this had happened and that it would never happen again. Once Burke had reassured him that there had been no complaints about quality, he insisted on walking his visitor through his business, ostensibly so that he could show the sketch to as many people as possible but, Burke couldn't help thinking, mainly to show off the quality of his produce. The place seemed clean and well-run and Burke did wonder how the maggots had got into the beef but he supposed these things happened even in the best regulated businesses.

None of the places he called on that afternoon had lost members of staff recently in mysterious circumstances. Nobody recognised the picture he showed them either. Two had recently taken on a new worker but in both cases it was someone who had come recommended by a current employee. In summary, as he complained to William that evening, he had come up with no leads at all.

"I want you back picking up servants' gossip, though. Concentrate on Morais and Carvalho. I want to know everything there is to know about those two. And while you concentrate on the chatter below stairs, I'm going to see what I can glean from their friends."

He started that night. It had been a while since he had been able to accept one of the dinner invitations that he got increasingly often from what passed for Society in Lisbon but that night he was a guest at the table of the Marquis of Arraiolos, one of the most senior aristocrats left in Portugal after the evacuation of the court to Brazil. The Marquis, unlike so many of Burke's new friends in Lisbon, was a strong supporter of the British Army and his guests were full of talk of how the campaign in Spain was going. There were lots of mentions of how splendid the victory at Talavera had been and Burke was careful not to disillusion them.

"But what I want to know," demanded one man in the uniform of one of the top Portuguese cavalry regiments, "is when Wellington is going to thrash the French bastards again. You can't win a war without taking the fight to the enemy."

There was a general rumble of agreement around the table, which at least reassured Burke that Wellington's plan to fall back behind the Lines was not common knowledge. Fletcher's careful security seemed to be holding up so far.

Morais and Carvalho were not among those invited. Over after-dinner drinks (not port, which was produced to survive the journey to England), Burke asked after them. "Haven't seen either of them for a while: wondered if they'd be here tonight." There were some dark looks and a viscount from a place so obscure that even his friends teased him about it took him aside and explained. The Marquis, it appeared was not a fan of either Morais or Carvalho. "This is a dinner for those who truly respect the efforts that England makes on our behalf. The gentlemen you mentioned would not really fit in." This was hardly news but it did give him the opportunity to ask more directly about his two chief suspects.

The gossip about Morais and his friend was far from damning but added to Burke's feeling of unease. He knew, of course, that the two had little patience with the English. But it was news that they were known to have communication with the French through military friends who (like a depressing number of Portuguese officers) has taken their men across to march under French colours during the occupation. "Not that they would ever betray their country," he was told, "but they may be indiscreet, so they are not entirely trusted by a loyalist like the marquis."

Burke muttered something vague and reassuring, but he was not reassured at all. There was nothing here to hang the two for treachery but, in an ideal world, he would welcome a quiet couple of hours with them in an out-of-the way prison cell. Sadly, the political sensitivities of the situation meant that methods that had been an everyday reality during his time in Ireland were not available to him now.

He thought of the spy network that Britain operated to keep track of those at home whose loyalties, like those of Morais and Carvalho, were not entirely beyond question. There were a surprising number of radicals who harboured some sympathy for Napoleon and were anxious to see the war at an end. An army of spies followed them about, intercepted their mail and arranged for their meetings to be broken up. Here, though, there was just him and William. He would love to have the two followed and their mail intercepted but there was nobody to do it.

Or was there?

Burke thought of Batarda's comments about the probable role of the aristocracy in this plot. The young man was obviously interested in the business of tracking down the spies and, as one of Fletcher's men, his loyalty was unquestionable. He was not an aristocrat but he clearly came from a good family, he rode well and he was in the army

– all factors that meant he would fit in socially with the world inhabited by Morais and Carvalho.

The next morning he was in Fletcher's office bright and (for him) early. Fletcher heard his idea and, to his relief decided it was a good one. "I can spare Batarda. Most of the work that he's been involved in it is coming to an end now and he'd enjoy the opportunity to get out and do something more active."

Major Batarda was indeed enthusiastic about the idea, especially when Burke suggested that he would fit in more easily as a member of a prestigious cavalry regiment than as a mere militia officer.

"But how could such a thing be achieved?"

Burke assured him that for a colonel of the Queen's Royal Regiment on the staff of General Beresford, such a thing could be achieved very easily.

It wasn't that easy. He had to assure Beresford that Batarda would be able to assist when Burke was on other duties. As Burke had been on these 'other duties' one way and another for weeks, Beresford was enthusiastic about anything that would relieve him of the trouble of dealing with the local population and their continual complaints.

"But this Batarda fellow is a militia officer, isn't he? Not really quite up to snuff, is he?"

Burke explained that he had been detached from the militia to work directly to Colonel Fletcher. He was careful not to say what Batarda did for Fletcher, and Beresford didn't bother to ask. Burke suspected that the General had no idea who Fletcher was. "Batarda's role is hardly a militia post. It might be best if he was transferred to the regular army. Cavalry, I'd have thought."

He had the order drafted already. Beresford grunted and signed it.

He saw Batarda with the good news that afternoon. "Better get straight to your tailor. You'll want to be in the finery of a cavalryman as soon as you can."

There was an embarrassed shuffling and Burke realised the problem. Never mind – Gordon had given him funds for his secret work and a uniform for Batarda was as honest a use for them as any.

* * *

Saturday saw him visiting yet more merchants who supplied the forts.

Fletcher knew that word would get out that this merchant or that had a contract to supply a fort north of Lisbon but security would only be compromised if they realised how many forts there were and how the pieces of the jigsaw fitted together. Merchants, though, talk to each other so, to protect his secret, Fletcher not only spread his business across dozens of different firms but he chose businesses that were scattered across the city. Lisbon was not a particularly large town, but Burke felt he had walked every street in the place twice over by the end of the day and he had nothing to show for his efforts.

William Brown had been out until the small hours and had had no luck either. His best hope was Major Batarda and it would take a while for him to build up any useful contacts.

The next day, being Sunday, he decided to give himself a day of rest. In this staunchly Catholic city the merchants would be closed and socialising would centre on families. He had no desire to take up again the Catholicism of his youth and he had no regimental chaplain who would notice his absence from the Anglican service, so he had a day to himself. Normally, on a free day he would walk around the town but given how he had spent his Saturday he decided to lounge around the house and make some inroads into a book of Walter Scott's Scottish ballads. He had brought it with him in the vague hope of improving his mind, but it had yet to be opened.

After a few hours of reading, he dozed off. When he awoke, his mind might not have been improved but it was rested. He ate a fine dinner with Snr Lopez and, despite his afternoon nap, retired to bed where he slept soundly until wakened by William the next morning.

Unlike him, William had not taken the day off on Sunday. Given that servants traditionally had a half day on the Sabbath, it was the most productive time to tackle footmen and upper servants. While maids knew their masters' habits – when they were in, when they were out, if their rooms showed that they did not sleep alone when their wives were out of town – it was the upper servants who were more likely to know who they plotted with, who they wrote to and if there was incriminating correspondence left in carelessly unlocked drawers.

"It's like you say, sir," William reported. "Things don't seem quite right but there's nothing you can put your finger on. Morais' men are loyal but they can get a bit careless after drink. They tap their noses and make out that they know great secrets, which they may but they're not sharing them. Carvalho's servants are more chatty with hints that he knows more Frenchmen than he's letting on. It's nothing we could arrest him for, though at a pinch we might arrest his under-butler and see what he tells us after an hour or two locked in a small room with me and a big stick."

Tempting as William's idea was, Burke had to veto it. "We have to tread carefully round these fellows and that includes their servants. We can't afford to have them openly turn against us. And if they are secretly turned against us, we must deal with it quietly and without scandal. Remember that our army is here to support the brave struggle of the Portuguese people. That's the story and nothing we do must suggest otherwise."

At least Batarda understood the sensitivities at play – but that meant that he was moving very slowly and carefully. It could be a while before he had anything useful to contribute. Burke took him to Beresford's headquarters where he was paraded in front of the general just long enough to ensure (Burke hoped) that Beresford would remember him if he saw him again. After that, he was introduced to the office that would be Burke's, if Burke ever spent any time there. The clerk was summoned and asked if there was anyone looking for an appointment.

In the time Burke had been away quite a few people had wanted appointments, although all had been turned away. "I tried to arrange meetings with General Beresford, sir, but either they didn't want to see him or he didn't want to see them so..." The clerk ground to a halt.

"Very good," said Burke – though clearly it wasn't. "Get a messenger and tell them all that Major Batarda is assisting while I am unavoidably detained. Make sure they know he has my full confidence and then line them up to see him."

Batarda looked overwhelmed at this sudden responsibility, but in the privacy of his office Burke assured him that he would definitely be able to cope.

"Be nice to them. You need to win their confidence. Get them to talk to you. If it's a simple problem, just deal with it. If it's not straightforward say that you will speak to me about it. We'll meet up once a day and we can sort things out. If you think they are being unreasonable — and some of them are – say that you will pass it on to General Beresford and then forget all about it."

"Do I pass it on to the General?"

"There's no real point. He has no interest at all in what these people have to say. That's why I was able to get you the job."

It was not, perhaps, the most thorough briefing that Burke had ever given to a man under his command, but it seemed to cover everything that mattered. Anyway, he had every confidence that Batarda was a bright young officer and that he would cope.

* * *

Burke spent the morning in more fruitless visits to merchants and the afternoon on the outskirts of the city where men who didn't have to work for a living were enjoying a horse race. Carvalho was there and Burke took the opportunity to talk to him without Morais around. They chatted about the merits of the horses that provided the entertainment. Carvalho knew a lot about horseflesh and was a lively conversationalist on the subject. Burke was careful not to bring up the subject of politics and nothing Carvalho said suggested that he was seriously interested in anything beyond the breeding and training of horses. Burke had to admit that he quite liked the man. Perhaps he had simply fallen into bad company with Morais, but, in the end, that made him no less potentially dangerous.

At the end of the afternoon he returned to see how Batarda was getting on and was relieved to discover that the clerk had managed to persuade two men to call in with their concerns and Batarda had acquitted himself well. They had been quite easily dealt with – the difficult customers would keep him waiting before they deigned to see him – but these were the first aristocratic contacts he had made and he was happy that he had given a good impression. It would be a while yet, though, before he was invited into their world – even on the fringes.

Tuesday passed quietly. Burke made only a couple of calls that morning. The first was to one of the smaller businesses where a harassed owner barely glanced at the picture between dealing with customers. The second was to a flourishing wholesaler whose owner, conscious of the value of his army contracts, had coffee served while he looked carefully at the pictures and called in various of his supervisors to confirm that nobody knew the man. Despite the hospitality, Burke found the visit depressing. He seemed to be wasting time and shoe leather in a wild goose chase. Was this man even involved with shipping goods to the Lines? Best wait, perhaps for Marta to produce sketches of more possible conspirators.

He spent that evening drinking with some wealthy young men who, after the first few glasses, praised the French loudly and effusively. Bonaparte was the sort of ruler who made a country great! He led his troops from the front: he did not skulk away the other side of the Atlantic when there was real fighting to be done. Burke was not worried about them. They were full of noise and fury but they weren't about to risk their comfortable lives, let alone their necks, to help the French. Instead he watched the men who nodded quietly but said nothing. He made a mental note of their names and added them to the growing list of possible traitors.

What he needed was solid evidence. If only Cristiano had been taken alive. With him dead, his best chance of success was Marta's sketches. If they could only get a picture of the third conspirator. Tonight, he supposed, might change that. He raised his glass to his lips and wondered if William was having any luck at *A Tendinha.*

CHAPTER 11: Not a good night out

As Burke was enjoying a fine wine with well-heeled company, William was coming to terms with the drink available to the poor at *A Tendinha*. At least he had better company. Marta, flushed with success after her last outing to the tavern, chattered happily as she sketched random faces that appealed to her.

William, sitting opposite, could only see them upside down, but even like that it was clear that she had real talent. Here she caught someone's roguish grin, there the glint of malice in a stranger's eye.

After an hour or so her busy hand stilled. "They've arrived, haven't they," said William without turning round.

Marta nodded and, taking up a new sheet of paper, she started drawing William, who held his pose – an ideal artist's model.

If anyone had notice her sketching the other customers earlier, all they would see now would be a girl concentrating on drawing the man opposite.

She finished her first effort and told him to change position so she could make an attempt on his profile. They'd been a while by now and William was beginning to wonder if Morais and Carvalho were going to be joined by anyone else when Marta again stopped mid-sketch to pick up another sheet of paper.

"This is someone new," she said.

So, William thought, four spies, not three.

"We'll add him to your portrait collection."

Marta started drawing. "There's something different about this one. He looks cross and he doesn't seem as –" She paused, searching for the word. "As deferential as the others. The aristos look upset at what they're hearing too."

William risked a glance. The man was on his feet and clearly angry. He leaned forward, speaking softly but almost spitting his words at Morais. Morais looked about to get to his feet himself, but Carvalho put a restraining hand on his arm and Morais immediately redirected his anger from the stranger to his sidekick. William could imagine how furious he would have felt: Carvalho daring to lay a hand on him. Even if Carvalho had saved him from unpleasantness. The stranger had an air about him that suggested that had things got physical – and they might well have – Morais could have ended up the victim of another bar-room brawl. Fortunately for him, while he was berating Carvalho the other man turned on his heel and pushed out of the tavern.

William could not be sure what had happened but one thing was for certain: no money had changed hands this evening.

"Do we give up?" asked Marta.

"We'll give it a while yet."

Marta turned back to her sketching but her heart was no longer in it. After watching her make a few listless strokes, William suggested another glass of wine from their ever-attentive waitress. William, like James, took care to tip well and the smile she gave him suggested that she would be more than willing to spend some time with him for a few reais more. Fortunately Marta did not see that smile but sipped at her wine until the waitress had gone and William was able to entertain her with stories of a soldier's life and his adventures on the road.

She had started to relax when William heard the moving of stools and general shifting around that happened when Morais and Carvalho wanted space made for a new guest. Marta nodded to confirm the arrival of a stranger. "It's neither of the men I saw before." Already her hand was moving and William watched the features of another man appearing on the paper.

"That's good," he said.

"Be quiet. I'm concentrating."

A minute later the sketch was finished and she was starting on another, catching the animation and excitement on the stranger's face.

"They're passing him money I think."

William didn't move. If Marta thought they were passing him money, that was good enough for him. What was important now was to draw no attention until Morais and Carvalho were safely out of the place and Marta could slip away with the drawing they had come to get.

William sat still with his back to the room while Marta started another sketch of him. He was relaxed but aware of movement behind him. He waited for the sound of a stool being pushed back in the area where the conspirators were sitting but he heard only the clink of glasses, the murmur of conversation and the sound of the door opening and shutting behind him.

Suddenly, Marta tensed, her eyes widening in fear.

"Well look who I've found!"

The voice from the doorway was horribly familiar. William turned slowly to see the grinning face of Johnny.

"You and your soldier friend too."

Behind him, three of Johnny's mates were crowding through the door.

"Still pretending you can draw." Johnny was already pushing through the crowd towards where William and Marta were sitting. "You little whore."

William started to his feet. Four to one was not good odds, but he was confident he could take them. It meant there was no possibility of leaving quietly though. In fact he could see Morais out of the corner of his eye. He was standing, watching what was developing and obviously listening to everything that Johnny was saying.

"You and your damn pictures."

Johnny made to swerve around William and grab at Marta's neatly piled stack of finished sketches. William was tensing for the uppercut which he had decided would start the fight when Morais appeared at their table and reached for the pictures before Johnny could grab them.

Morais' arrival postponed the start of the brawl. Though he had no patience for the aristocracy, William found himself deferring to his simple assumption of superiority. Hundreds of years of breeding and the obsequious submission of others to his demands meant that it was second nature to him to take charge of the situation.

He picked up the sketch she was working on, glancing between the picture and William's face.

"It's very good," he said. He turned to Marta. "You know, my dear, I've been looking for someone who can draw like you. I've heard of some very good sketches that are being shown to some of the leading merchants around the town. They were so impressed that they sent word back to me. Would you know anything about this?"

Marta looked like a rabbit facing a fox. Slowly she shook her head.

Morais dropped the picture of William and reached for the next. Desperately, William tried to grab up the papers. Before he could though, his arm was held in an iron grip. Carvalho had joined the group around the table and had taken hold of William who could do nothing but protest. “They’re not for you. She drew them for me. Leave her alone.”

He could hear the panic and despair in his own voice. Seldom had he felt so helpless.

Morais picked up the next sheet and raised it to his face. As he realised what he was looking at, his expression grew suddenly hard.

“Why did you draw a picture of this man?”

Marta stared at him, struck dumb with terror.

“She drew pictures of lots of the men here. She does it for fun. Look, you can see.” Carvalho was still holding his right arm but William reached with his left, scattering the papers, showing all the sketches Marta had drawn while they were waiting for Morais and Carvalho to turn up.

Morais glanced down at them.

“Perhaps,” he admitted. “But I think she should still come with us to answer some questions.”

He took her arm and, her face still a mask of terror, Marta began to get to her feet.

William tried to rise but the grip on his arm tightened. He jerked forward and then reversed the move, slamming his elbow into Carvalho’s stomach. Carvalho released his grip and William was up and reaching for Morais, but at that moment Johnny decided to join in the fight.

William’s head was struck from behind and he span around, half stunned. Marta screamed and William saw Morais pulling her towards the door, but he could do nothing until he had finished with Johnny. Stunned as he was, he still threw a punch that had Johnny stagger back into the arms of his friends.

He had discounted Carvalho, who hardly seemed a fighting man, but the aristocrat was tougher than William had expected. Once he had recovered enough to stand up, instead of taking to his heels with Morais, he made a short, vicious jab into William’s cheek. The unexpected blow from the side distracted William for the moment that it took for Johnny's friends the chance to pile in.

William's eyes were already swelling and his view of Morais was blurring as the aristocrat turned to follow Morais out of the tavern. William saw light glitter on the coin he threw towards Johnny.

"Finish him," he said.

William managed one more solid blow at the first of Johnny's friends and then he was on the ground and they were kicking and all was blood and pain. Above him were four faces, as much animal as human. He expected no mercy, but suddenly there was a fifth face and he heard the waitress.

"Enough, lads. Sit down and I'll get you drinks."

They didn't sit down at once, of course. They could not allow themselves to be seen as taking orders from a woman. But the kicks became more desultory and, after a couple of minutes, the prospect of free wine became more attractive and they drifted away.

James was right, William thought. Always tip the waitress before a bar fight.

He tried to get up from the floor, but his legs didn't seem to be working.

He fell back and everything went black.

* * *

A Tendinha had not struck William as a place which was overly concerned with how clean its floor was, but it turned out but they mopped it religiously every morning. William discovered this when a bucket of dirty water was dumped unceremoniously on his head where he lay in the street outside the tavern.

His first thought was gratitude that he was not dead. Everything hurt, but cautious movement of all four limbs suggested that nothing was actually broken. As he struggled to his feet the pain in his chest suggested at least a couple of cracked ribs and he could barely see out of his right eye. No matter: he would be able to make it home with one eye.

He took a cautious step and staggered. His legs were so bruised that it was agony to put his weight onto them. He took another step and lurched against the wall, leaning on it for support.

There were no sedan chairs for hire in Lisbon. Here in Alfama, with its narrow steep lanes, there were hardly any carts. In any case, William had no money to pay for his transport home. Whoever had thrown his unconscious body onto the street had emptied his pockets first. There was no help for it. Step by agonising step he set off to walk to Snr Lopez's house.

CHAPTER 12: Marta's story

I saw Sgt Brown go down. He tried to save me but he was struck from behind and then they were all hitting him and he fell and I couldn't see him anymore.

I wanted to stay. I wanted to help him, but I was just a girl. What could I have done?

In any case, I was dragged outside before I could do anything, but once on the street, I did what any sensible girl would do. I screamed.

It did no good at all. I suppose people often hear women screaming outside taverns like that. All I managed to do was annoy the man who still had me by the arm.

"Shut up!" he said to me. He tried to slap me, but he was still holding my drawings in that hand so he ended up just hitting me with sheets of paper, which would have been funny if I hadn't been so frightened. His friend followed him out and he took his temper out on him.

"What the hell do we do with her? We need to find out what she knows."

That was my cue. "I don't know anything. Let me go!"

They both ignored me. The man holding my arm thought for a moment and then said back, "We'll take her to your place in the country." His friend didn't look too happy with the idea but the first man didn't seem to care. "Your carriage is waiting at the bottom of the hill," he said. "We just have to get her down there."

My captor pulled at my arm but by now I had recovered from the initial shock and I stuck in my heels and kept screaming. It was a waste of effort and breath. His friend just slapped me. He wasn't holding papers in his hand. He slapped me hard. It hurt. I stopped screaming and followed where I was led.

There were a few people on the street as we walked downhill. I cried out to some of them, but I suppose they just saw some tavern girl who had sold herself and was now having second thoughts. I heard some of them laugh. None of them helped.

We arrived at the carriage. It had a coat of arms on the door. It was obviously owned by somebody rich. There was a coachman and a liveried servant. The two men bundled me inside and got in with me. The coachman and the servant just watched.

"The hunting lodge!" the man who had grabbed me said, and the coach rolled off.

We drove for a long time, well out of the town, rattling along country roads in the dark. They did not do anything to me but I was scared. They sat there, grim and silent. I think they were scared themselves, which made me even more frightened. Men who are scared can do terrible things and I was completely at their mercy.

We stopped at last in front of a house on its own in the middle of nowhere. I suppose this was what he had called 'the hunting lodge', but it didn't look like a hunting lodge. It was difficult to see what it looked like in the dark, but it was a big place, two floors high and not at all what I thought 'hunting lodge' meant.

We obviously weren't expected, but when the carriage arrived I saw lights appearing in the windows and suddenly there were servants hurrying out to meet us. I was taken out of the carriage and two footmen took me by the arms and let me into the building. What could I do? Even if I could have escaped -- and they were big men who did not look as if they would be sympathetic to my struggles – where would I have gone? They took me to a bedroom, pushed me in, and locked the door behind me.

If I had not been a prisoner, with no idea of what was planned for me, I would have been so delighted with that room. It was the most luxurious room I had ever seen. The floor was of wood but most of it was covered by a beautiful carpet with red and blue flowers, but not like any pictures of flowers I'd ever seen before. They looked foreign and exotic. The walls were not bare stone, like I'm used to, but covered in paper and there was a painting of a stag. There was a dressing table with a huge mirror and some chairs that looked as if they would break if you actually sat on them. And, of course, there was a bed with a blue silk cover over it. I pressed down on it and it was so soft I could hardly believe it. In my present predicament, though, the comfort provided by a featherdown mattress counted for little.

I was left alone with my thoughts for – well, in truth I know not how long. It seemed like hours, but the candles had hardly burned down at all so I imagine it cannot have been that many minutes.

The two men came back in. Both were quite tall and in different circumstances I might have thought them handsome. Both had dark hair but one was naturally quite curly while the other wore his brushed down flat to his head. Perhaps he was used to wearing a wig over it. You don't see many wigs in my part of Lisbon, but I know some of the rich gentlemen still wear them.

They obviously were gentlemen – or, at least, people would call them gentlemen. It wasn't only the big house and the carriage. It was the way they behaved as if they knew that, whatever it was that they wanted, they were going to get. It was only a matter of time.

What they wanted from me was to know what I was doing at *A Tendinha* and the name of the soldier I was doing it with.

I told them the truth: I was there to sketch the men they were talking to. They had the drawings with them – it was pointless to lie. "But he asked me to draw a lot of other men too."

He hadn't, of course. I'd drawn them for my own satisfaction but they will not know that.

Curly – I might as well call him that for neither ever revealed their names – picked out a picture of Sgt Brown. What was his name, he wanted to know. I remembered how Colonel Burke had said I was to call him Bob, so I said his name was Bob and that I didn't know his last name.

Curly turned to his friend and said, "You can pass round this picture. That should help us find him – if he's still alive to be found." His friend nodded and took the paper. I think Curly is the boss of the two and his friend does what he is told.

I didn't like the sound of that 'If he's still alive to be found.' I liked Sgt Brown and I would be sorry if anything had happened to him.

"Why did he want the pictures?"

I shrugged. I tried very hard to look as if it seemed of no importance to me. "I don't know," I said. "Maybe he wanted to surprise his friends."

Curly's expression suggested he did not think this was very likely.

"How much did he pay you?"

"A hundred reals," I said. If I told him how much I was really being paid, they would never believe I was just an innocent caught up in this.

"She doesn't know anything," Curly's friend said. "We should let her go."

This should have made me feel more sympathetic to Curly's friend, but it only made me despise him even more. He seemed weak. In any case, Curly didn't agree with him.

"We don't know anything about her. We need to find this soldier she was with and question him. And we need to know what the two of them were up to. Who is she and where does she come from?" He turned to me. He didn't even bother asking me the question – he just waited for me to answer.

I had to tell him the truth. If I lied, they would find out soon enough and I would be in even more trouble. I told him my name and where I lived. "But please, sir, tell my mother I am alright. She will be frightened that I have not come home."

He didn't reply – just turned to his friend and told him that he should send somebody to check that my story was true. Then, without another word, he turned and left the room.

His friend stood there looking uncomfortable. He really was pathetic, I decided.

"I'm sorry, senhorita," he said at last. "You will need to stay here for a while. I will give orders to the servants to ensure that you are comfortable."

He opened and shut his mouth a few more times as if trying to think of something else to say and then he just sort of shuffled out. I heard the key turn in the lock.

CHAPTER 13: Find the lady

Burke had never known William late with his morning tea. Whatever hour he had finished carousing in the local bars the night before, he would always arrive as Burke woke, teapot, milk jug, cup and saucer carefully arranged on a tray. He never knew how he did it. Did he lurk outside the bedroom listening for signs of Burke's awakening? That seemed unlikely. He just put it down to William's near-magical powers which had somehow transformed a child of the slums into a perfect valet – as well as a remarkably good spy.

He was worried, then, when there was no sign of William when he woke. Breakfast came and went and there was still no Sgt Brown. Enquiries in the servants' hall revealed that nobody had seen him since he set off for Marta's home the previous evening. Burke even ventured up into the attic to discover that Brown's bed had not been slept in.

It seemed a visit to Marta's house was called for, but at that moment a commotion at the front door revealed Brown being helped into the house by a stranger in workman's clothing. It turned out to be a builder who, on his way to one of the grand houses with some marble for the finishing touches to the façade, had come across Brown dragging himself along the road and taken pity on him.

The Good Samaritan had carried Brown in his cart out of the goodness of his heart but Burke insisted on a generous payment while Snr Lopez had the man taken to the servant's hall to be plied with food and drink before being allowed to go about his business.

Other servants had descended on William to carry him off to bed. William tried to swipe them away but Burke told him not to be silly. "I will join you as soon as you are settled and you will tell me your story then. You are clearly in no condition to do anything other than talk at present and you can talk as easily in your bed as anywhere else."

Burke allowed ten minutes for William to be put to bed before he shooed an over-solicitous house maid out of the room and sat to hear his sergeant's report.

He was quiet while William spoke and sat in silence at the end of the sorry tale.

"It seems," he said eventually, "that I should pay Snr Morais a visit."

"I don't know that will help, sir. There's nobody going to admit to his having been there. He abducts a girl and has me beaten unconscious and nobody in the joint does anything." He winced. Even speaking was painful, Burke noticed. "It must be nice to have that sort of power."

"He still has Marta, William. We can't simply ignore him."

"She could be dead, sir."

Sometimes Burke wished William was not quite so realistic in his assessment of life. He did not want to consider the possibility that Marta was dead while there was any hope at all of finding her alive. And a good starting point for finding her alive would be Morais' house. Perhaps the simplest way would be to gather up a dozen or so soldiers, kick in his front door and search the place from top to bottom.

He had expected the idea to cheer William but, to his surprise, it did not.

"She won't be there. All you'll have done is warn him that we're watching him and will never be able to prove anything. We won't be able to do anything about his spying and we still won't have found Marta."

"If she's not at his house, where else would she be?"

William eased himself into a more comfortable position on the bed. "Those evenings I spent drinking with his staff weren't entirely wasted," he said. "They mentioned the little palace the family owns up near Porto and the house he keeps his mistresses in. He's between women at the moment, so that's empty. Or, of course, she could be at one of Carvalho's places. Or dead in a ditch."

William, Burke admitted, was being more realistic than him. There was every chance that they would never find Marta and if they did it was not evidence that Morais and Carvalho were spies. Abducting the girl was a crime, of course, but it would be presented as high-spirited foolishness by two young men. Marta would be dismissed as a whore. Some money might make its way to her home, but that would be small comfort after her reputation had been destroyed. Morais and Carvalho would know they were being watched and Burke would lose any chance of infiltrating the spy network through them. How could he explain to Gordon that he had abandoned his mission because of his concerns for this girl?

In the end, his first duty was to Gordon and his efforts to thwart a French plot. But was there a way to save Marta without endangering his mission? Perhaps there was.

"If she's not dead, she must have been taken from Alfama. Morais could not have a bolt-hole there. He'd stick out like a sore thumb. And she can't have been led through the streets of Lisbon. You might be able to manhandle a girl through Alfama but it would certainly draw attention once you were in more respectable areas. So my guess is a coach."

William nodded.

"So we need to find out which of them had a coach on the road last night and where it went. That's exactly the sort of thing you're so good at wheedling out of the servants."

"Well, I'm no use for that now. It's a bit too obvious that I'm the idiot that got beaten up when Marta was taken. I can't do my job when everybody knows who I am."

There was a silence while they contemplated the extent of their failure.

"Of course," said William, "you only really need to talk to the stable staff."

"I can hardly turn up at Morais' stables and demand to know if they used the coach last night."

More silence. Burke felt that there was an answer tantalisingly close. Maybe he should try talking to Batarda. Perhaps that young officer might have an idea.

And then, he had a sudden inspiration.

"You're a genius, William. You stay and rest and I'll find out what the stable staff know."

CHAPTER 14: A rescue party

Major Batarda was only one man but Colonel Fletcher had more where he came from and Fletcher seemed to Burke to be a man who would be prepared to bend the rules when the life of a young woman was in danger.

When Burke explained his plan, Fletcher was positively enthusiastic and that afternoon half a dozen of his guards left his headquarters to help in the search for Marta. Smartly uniformed in the red coats they had abandoned under Fletcher's command, they appeared in the stable yards of several members of the local nobility.

They were employed, they explained to the head groom, on a project essential to the war effort. They could go into no details, such was the secrecy involved, but they were anxious to obtain information about carriages for a special mission. There was no question, of course, of requisitioning vehicles from such important households, but it would be of invaluable assistance if they knew how much carriages in houses such as theirs were being used. For example, had the carriages been driven out in the past week? The soldier would note the reply and go on with other questions until, without appearing to have shown particular interest in any specific day, they knew which households had carriages out the previous night.

Colonel Fletcher's obsession with secrecy and security appeared to have turned his men into natural agents. How often did these carriages go out at night? How far did they generally travel? How far last night, for example?

By the end of the day, Fletcher knew that Morais' carriage had been in the stables all night. Carvalho's, on the other hand, had been out until that morning.

"My man asked if the horse coped well being driven for such a long time," Fletcher explained to Burke. "The groom said that they had been rested for hours. They'd journeyed ten miles to the lodge, he said. And ten miles back in the morning."

"He said 'the lodge'?" asked Burke.

"My man wrote it down. He suggested it might be important. Is he right?"

"He's right," said Burke. "Now all we have to do is break into Snr Carvalho's hunting lodge and get the girl out."

"You'd be welcome to my fellows. They're not stupid. They've worked out more or less what this is about and once you tell them there's a maiden in distress at this lodge, they'll be keen to get stuck in."

"I was thinking of something more subtle. I want the girl out without Morais knowing we know. As if she'd escaped by herself."

"Good luck with that! I take it that your Sgt Brown isn't going to be in any position to assist you."

Burke confirmed that Brown wouldn't be breaking damsels out of the lairs of evil villains for a while.

"You should take Batarda," said Fletcher. "He'll enjoy that."

* * *

Batarda had arranged horses. "That's the advantage of being in the cavalry," he said. "Lovely mounts."

In Burke's view there was no time to lose so they had set off in time to arrive at the lodge soon after dark.

They got lost of course. There were no decent maps and they had only the vaguest idea where the wretched lodge was. They arrived around one in the morning which Batarda pointed out was probably a good thing as at one o'clock everyone was likely to be sound asleep.

There was no sign of sentries and the house was in darkness. Burke might have thought that the place was deserted and they had come on a fool's errand but he could smell smoke. It was too warm for the fires to have been made-up so that suggested smoke from the kitchen and that meant there were staff there – not only a housekeeper or caretaker. A solitary servant would have been expected to make do with bread and cheese.

Carvalho and Morais were back in Lisbon. It had been easy enough to check that during the nonsense with the survey of coaches. Burke hoped that it meant Marta was here.

The door was locked, so Burke simply broke a window. Pushing out a small pane of glass made hardly a sound. He doubted anyone would have noticed even if they had been awake. He reached through, unlatched the window and the two of them were in.

Burke lit a candle. The danger of the light being seen seemed much less serious than the likelihood of them crashing into something in the dark.

They were in an entrance hall – not especially grand but big enough for the decorative suits of armour to look quite natural. The smell of smoke was stronger inside the house. He turned his head and sniffed. The kitchens were at the back as he would have expected. He glanced inside. There was no door leading to a cellar. He supposed that a cellar was considered unnecessary in a hunting lodge, though he suspected the building saw more feasting than it saw humble suppers after a day of killing deer.

If there was no cellar and Marta was here, then she was presumably upstairs.

Burke had noticed back stairs running from the kitchen. These would enable the servants to service the bedrooms without using the main staircase: that was reserved for the owner and his guests. The servants' stairs would probably run on up to an attic floor where they had their bedrooms. Should they search for Marta on that attic floor or in the guest bedrooms on the first floor?

Burke decided to start with the guest bedrooms. Carvalho was definitely not in the lodge and it seemed likely that Marta was the only person there besides the servants. He should be able to check the guest bedrooms without any real danger of opening the door on somebody who would raise the alarm. Of course, she might be in the attic, which would mean having to deal with the servants, but that was a problem to worry about only after they were sure she wasn't on the floor below.

Burke and Batarda started up the stairs. It was more like the staircase of a grand house than a humble hunting lodge, which was all to the good as it meant that the stairs did not creak.

On the first floor, a corridor ran the length of the house, five bedrooms leading off on either side. Obviously Carvalho liked to entertain.

Burke listened carefully at the first door. Silence. Slowly he turned the doorknob and eased the door open. Not a sound. Stepping into the room he raised his candle. The place was empty.

Nine more rooms to go.

While Burke had listened at the first door, Batarda, with what Burke felt was the impatience of youth, had moved on down the corridor. Now, as Burke moved out of the first room, Batarda touched him on the shoulder and gestured ahead.

Burke followed as Batarda led him past three more rooms and pointed to the last door.

There was a key in the lock.

Burke nodded his thanks and gently turned the key and eased the door open. A single candle flickered on the mantelpiece, providing enough light to see Marta sound asleep in her bed.

"Thank God," Burke whispered and beside him he glimpsed Batarda crossing himself.

Burke stepped close to the bed. "Marta." He spoke softly, ready to put his hand across her mouth if she woke in a panic and screamed but she did not.

The girl turned, stretched and opened her eyes.

"Colonel Burke," she said. "I was hoping you would find me." And then, seeing Batarda in the shadows, "But this is not Sgt Brown." Her eyes widened. "Is your sergeant alright? When they took me, he …" Her voice trailed away.

"He is hurt, senhorita but he will recover. This is Major Batarda, who is assisting me in Sgt Brown's absence." The major bowed. "But now we have to get you out of here. You need to dress yourself."

The two men stood guard at the door, carefully turning away from Marta as she prepared herself for leaving the room. The pause gave Burke time to think. They could relock the door and slip away, leaving her captors to puzzle out what had happened, but they were unlikely to believe that she had spirited herself out of the lodge without assistance. He wanted Morais blissfully unaware of how closely he was being watched. Best create some sort of confusion in which Marta could perhaps have made her own escape.

He glanced back into the room. The candle still flickered on the mantlepiece. But perhaps Marta might have taken it to stand by the bed because she was frightened alone there in a strange house. And perhaps it could have fallen against the bedclothes as she slept.

That, Burke decided, was the answer. It might not work but with luck it would burn the building down and that would at least give him the satisfaction of imagining Carvalho's face when he learned the news. It would be even more satisfying if it were Morais' lodge, for Burke was sure he was the leader of the two, but he would settle for what he could get.

Once Marta was dressed, Batarda led her down the corridor while Burke started the fire in her room.

Nobody woke to challenge them as they hurried down the stairs.

Outside, Burke glanced behind him as they headed for where they had left the horses. The blaze he had started was well alight and flames were leaping from the window. He heard cries of alarm. The servants must be awake, but he doubted they would be able to stop the fire now.

The three of them moved silently into the trees. Marta mounted pillion with Batarda, sacrificing modesty to the need to make a quick getaway. Burke followed as they rode easily back to Lisbon.

CHAPTER 15: Marta saves the day

Arriving at Snr Lopez's home with two strangers in the small hours of the morning was not the behaviour of a well-mannered guest but Snr Lopez was no fool. He must have realised by now that Colonel Burke's business was not conventional soldiering.

William was woken. A day of rest had left him still battered but not so damaged that he did not want to join them to reassure himself that Marta was safe and she, in turn, was delighted to see him. He vanished for a while to make arrangements for her to share a room with one of the maids. It was not an ideal arrangement but it met the requirements of propriety without waking Snr Lopez to sort out his new houseguest.

The three men gathered in Burke's room to plan their next step.

"We need Marta somewhere safe and secluded. Given how quickly the fire took hold, it's quite possible they think she burned to death and it's safest for her if they continue to think that. We can't keep her here. It's too obvious and it ties her to me if she's seen. She can't go home. Any suggestions?"

There was a pause and then Batarda spoke. "My mother lives in Lisbon. She could stay with her."

It turned out that Batarda's mother lived in a quiet area on the edge of town. Marta could stay there with no danger of stumbling into Morais or any of his allies. "My mother is a great patriot. She would be proud to help us."

That immediate problem having been sorted out, it left the rather more intractable issue of what to do about Morais and Carvalho. Batarda was all in favour of arresting them or – failing that – simply grabbing them on the street and bundling them off to a quiet cellar where Batarda said he would be happy to beat them until he had no secrets left to confess. It seemed that in the hours he had spent on his horse with Marta pressed against his back, he had conceived enough affection for the girl to feel that beating the two men who had threatened her was the only way that an honourable gentleman could behave. Burke was almost certain that he heard the word 'horsewhip' mentioned.

Burke could remember when he was younger and would have taken much the same approach but, as he explained, they had to be more cautious. "We suspect that a man was murdered so that Cristiano could get his job. Does that sound like something Morais and Carvalho could organise by themselves? And where do they find these men they meet at *A Tendinha*? Do they seem the sort to consort with working men? And whose idea was it to meet at *A Tendinha*?" He turned to William. "The first thing you told me about that place was that it wasn't the sort of drinking hole where you would expect to find aristocrats like them. They wouldn't usually have any idea where it was, even if they knew it existed. No, there is more to this plot than Morais and Carvalho and we need to trace it back and strike at the head."

"That's easy enough to say, but how do we do that?" Batarda obviously still favoured an approach that featured a cellar and a length of lead piping.

"Possibly through the men that we saw at *A Tenhida*. If I'm right, they weren't recruited by those two. If we find out who recruited them, we are that much closer to establishing how this conspiracy was organised. Then we might be in a position to destroy it."

William grimaced. "I think we'd best not show our faces at *A Tenhida* again. After what happened to Martha and me, we're not going to be able to follow up anything in that place. Not unless we go in with half a dozen soldiers at our backs, and what will that achieve?"

There was a long silence at the end of which Burke suggested that they get what rest they could and worry about it the next morning.

William made his way back to his room while Batarda pulled off his boots and settled himself to sleep in Burke's armchair.

Burke had expected to lie awake a while worrying at the problem but he was actually asleep almost as soon as his head touched the pillow.

He was the first to wake the next morning – probably because his mattress had given him a better night's sleep than the chair where young Batarda was currently snoring.

As he stretched and contemplated the business of the day, he was astonished to hear a tap at the door and see William entering bearing a tea tray.

"Good God, man! What are you doing up? You should be resting."

"And miss out on the fun, sir?"

"I don't know that there's much fun to miss out on. I don't think we'll be any further on than we were last night."

William poured the tea. "I thought I could bring Miss Marta down to see if her experience produced anything of interest."

Burke shrugged. "I suppose it makes sense. It's improper, of course, for her to be in my room but with you and Batarda here to chaperone her…"

Batarda's snoring had stopped and at the sound of his name he sat up, yawning.

"Would you like tea, sir?" asked William.

Batarda gave him a look that left him in no doubt that Portuguese officers did not drink tea in the morning.

"I'll get you some coffee, sir."

William vanished, leaving Burke sipping his tea and Batarda looking astonished.

"Is he like that every morning?"

Burke nodded.

"Where did you find him?"

"Initially, in Sainte Domingue, but that was a very long time ago."

Batarda said nothing but concentrated on pulling on his boots.

There was another tap on the door and William entered, balancing a tray with two cups of coffee while he ushered Marta in with the other hand.

Marta smiled at the three of them. "Good morning, Juan," she greeted Batarda, blushing a little as she spoke.

'Juan.' Burke realised that's until that moment he hadn't known the major's name. Obviously their time together on horseback had not been wasted.

After they had all exchanged greetings and sipped at their drinks, Burke summarised the conclusions they had come to the night before.

"So you see," he said to Marta, "we had good reason to ask you to visit *A Tendinha* again. We should never have put you in such danger and – as it turns out – without gaining anything from your efforts."

"But you can now show a drawing of the man you were looking for."

Burke smiled reassuringly. Her experiences had obviously resulted in her having only a confused recollection of what had happened. "I'm afraid, my dear, that we do not have the picture. It was taken from you when you were abducted."

"But what I have drawn once, I can draw again. The picture I drew the night before last is still clear in my memory."

The mood, which had been quite sombre, changed in an instant. William was out scouring the house for pencil and paper while James pushed aside his book of Scott's ballads (still unfinished) to make room for Marta to draw at his writing table.

On William's return, Marta was sat down at the desk with pencil and paper while they all clustered around to watch her draw.

"For heaven's sake, give me some space. I need to concentrate."

And concentrate she did. Her eyes closed, her brow furrowed in thought and then she opened her eyes and began to draw.

She drew for around five minutes before she seemed happy with her efforts. "It's not perfect, but I think it should do." She passed it to William. "What do you think?"

William's eyes lit with the sort of wonder Burke associated with a small boy being presented with a sweet that a magician had just produced out of the air. "It's amazing. He looked exactly like that!"

He passed it to Burke.

"I know that man." The others stared at him as he tried to remember where he had seen him. "He was at one of the provision merchants I visited." He closed his eyes, trying to remember which one. On the second day, he thought. Somewhere in the north of the city. An office; two or three clerks. One went to get the owner.

That was the man.

"Pereira and Sons. That's where I saw him."

* * *

William, predictably, was all in favour of turning up at Pereira and Sons, finding the man in the picture, and beating him until he revealed all he knew about the plot.

Burke sympathised. The plotters were the reason for William's cracked ribs and aching limbs. It was only natural that he should be out to seek revenge. But what, Burke asked, if the man didn't talk? Even if he did, with one of the spies taken up, might the others not scatter before the interrogation had finished? Better, surely, to take a subtler approach.

"I'll visit Pereira and Sons again and talk to Snr Pereira. I've shown him the pictures we've got of the second man, but I never showed him the picture of Cristiano given he was already dead and we knew where he came from. But if one of our spies works in his offices, he may know more than he's admitting. I'll show him Cristiano's picture and see how he reacts. And I can take a look around for our new friend while I'm there."

He took the horse Batarda had offered him. He was tired of tramping the streets of the city and he wasn't going to rush to return the beast to the cavalry's stables.

He made for the wholesaler while Batarda went to Marta's mother to assure her that her daughter was safe. It was a mission that Burke could not help but notice that Batarda was very enthusiastic about. Clearly he had already made a favourable impression on the girl and he now seemed anxious repeat the trick with her mother. Burke was pleased that this suggested his intentions were honourable. He felt the situation had left him *in loco parentis* to Marta and he really didn't want to have to take a horsewhip to the major.

In his red coat and mounted on a cavalry charger, Burke's arrival at Pereira and Sons turned heads, even in the apparent chaos of their courtyard. The firm was one of the largest he had visited in his perambulations around Lisbon and the courtyard was full of activity. On one side were the offices and on the other was stabling. Between them, forming the longest side, was a huge warehouse. Carts were continually rattling their way across the cobbles, stacked up with vegetables. In the time it took him to tie his horse to the hitching post outside the offices, Burke saw carrots, potatoes, cabbages and an array of other green comestibles he couldn't begin to identify. He saw no fish but the piscine odour that permeated so much of Lisbon was here too, suggesting that there were fish hidden away somewhere.

The yard was full of men coming and going. Porters pushed barrows; clerks strode self-importantly about, clutching sheaves of paper; stable boys rushed to harness and unharness the horses. Burke admired the organisation. Though people seemed to mill about aimlessly, a short man in an embroidered waistcoat directed traffic in and out of the warehouse, stopping some carts to check the goods they carried. He wore the waistcoat as if it were a uniform and Burke felt he had the air of the sort of NCO that made the army run as it should. By the stables, an older man seemed, despite his limp (a war wound, Burke imagined), to rule his little corner of the yard like a medieval monarch, striking out with a stick at any of the lads he thought was too slow.

Burke pushed his way through the crowd gathered at the office doors – many of them farmers from their clothes – and made his way to Snr Pereira's office. A clerk in the outer office glanced up from the ledger he was writing, took one look at his red coat, and hurried to show him in.

Pereira was sat at his desk – a huge oak affair with a leather top supported on elaborately carved lions' feet. It was clearly designed to impress visitors with the heritage and wealth of the business, but Burke refused to allow it to impress him. The desk said solid and reliable but Snr Pereira's appearance said nervous and disorganised. As he entered, Burke saw Pereira scrabbling for some papers so that he could be seen working purposefully away, but he succeeded only in knocking them to the ground and instead steepled his fingers in a way he obviously hoped would imply gravitas. Burke thought it was a good thing that he had such efficient men ordering the running of the yard. He suspected that Pereira probably relied on them to do most of the actual work of the business.

Burke produced the sketch of Cristiano. Did Pereira know this man?

Pereira glanced casually at the picture and then, it seemed to Burke, stiffened. He looked at it again. "It's possible he might have worked here. Let me ask my clerk." He raised his voice. "Angelo!"

Burke heard a stool scraped back in the outer office. Burke turned in his seat as Angelo entered. Fortunately he had schooled himself not to allow his feelings to show on his face but, taken unawares, it was all he could do not to react as he saw the third man Marta had drawn standing there behind him. It seemed for a moment that time stood still.

"Have we ever had this man working here?"

Pereira's question broke the spell. Angelo picked up the picture. Was there, Burke wondered, a hint of recognition in his eyes?

"I don't think so, senhor." He turned to Burke. "Who is this man?"

"There's a gang stealing from the provisions that are supposed to be sent to the militia units north of Lisbon. We wondered if he might be one of them."

Angelo looked at the picture again. "No, I definitely don't know him."

Burke heard the flat tone he used – the tone of someone carefully controlling his reaction. He was, Burke was certain, lying.

He put the paper back on Snr Pereira's desk. As he did so, Burke was sure he saw a glance between them. Unfortunately, you can't arrest people for a glance.

Angelo returned to his stool and Snr Pereira rose to show Burke out but Burke had no intention of leaving yet.

"I'm sorry to bother you further, senhor, but we are asking everyone who supplies the militia if we can have details of all their clerks. The level of theft is becoming a concern and we believe it can't be happening without the involvement of some of the clerks."

Snr Pereira, naturally enough, insisted that all his staff were above suspicion.

"Of course, senhor. But you must understand we have to ask for details from all the businesses involved so we can rule them out." That didn't seem to him to make a lot of sense, but it satisfied Snr Pereira. He drew a ledger down from the shelf and provided the names of the three clerks in the outer office and two who were engaged elsewhere,

"Your clerks' duties extend beyond the office?"

Yes, they did. Provisions were brought in from the markets and delivered directly from farms. The clerks were responsible for checking that the goods arriving matched those which had been ordered. "Sometimes we order sheep's cheese, for example, and somehow it gets garbled and goat's cheese is delivered." The clerks also checked that the goods met the firm's quality standards. Snr

Pereira talked for a while about the high quality standards that they worked to but Burke, who knew rather too much about the basis on which armies ordered their food supplies, paid little attention to this. What he did pay attention to, and what had his pencil busy scribbling in his notebook, was what checks were carried out before hiring these clerks.

"It sounds a very responsible job. Where do you find these paragons?"

"Some have been with the business in other capacities. Then we hire on the recommendation of existing staff. Sometimes an older clerk will suggest his son take over from him and, if the lad is smart enough, we will train him up." Snr Pereira smiled. "Clerking here can be almost like a hereditary title, passed down from father to son through the generations."

"And did you inherit the business from your father?"

"I did – and he from his."

"So you know the families of all the clerks here."

"Generally, yes."

"Any who are new to the business?"

"Only the one who you spoke to – Angelo. He joined us recently and it's been harder to find men since the war."

"So where did Angelo come from?"

"He was recommended by …" Snr Pereira seemed suddenly uncertain what to say. "A colleague," he finished, somewhat lamely in Burke's opinion.

"I'm sorry, senhor, but we need to check the references of all these people. As I say, there is a great deal of money at stake. So who recommended Angelo?"

Snr Pereira threw up his hands in exasperation. "It was a gentleman who has taken an interest in this business. He has an impeccable reputation and I was happy to accept his assurances about Angelo who has, in the year or so he has been with us, proven honest and reliable." He stood and placed his palms on the desk, leaning forward toward Burke. "Is that enough? Can I get on with my work now?"

Burke knew when to push and when to stop pushing. There was something definitely not quite right about the place – more than simply Angelo's links to Morais and Carvalho. Pereira, too, had something to hide. Best, he thought, to leave now and return when he knew more about Angelo, Snr Pereira and his mysterious colleague.

Bowing his thanks he left Snr Pereira's office. As he walked through the clerks' room outside, he could feel Angelo's eyes on this back.

He resolved to avoid dark alleys until he knew exactly what was going on.

* * *

Back in Snr Lopez's house, he was pleased to find Juan Batarda waiting there with William. "I've taken Marta to my mother's house but I thought I should come back here and see what our next move is to be."

They gathered together in the dining room. There was nobody else using it and it was nice to be able to sit around the table rather than perch wherever they could find space in Burke's bedroom.

Burke summarised what little he had learned at the provision merchant. "There's nothing obviously wrong there but some things looked odd. For one thing, the relationship between Snr Pereira and his clerk didn't seem quite right. I would have expected more deference, but the two of them gave me the impression that they were working together to pull the wool over my eyes. And when Angelo said that he had no idea who Cristiano was, I'm pretty sure he was lying. I want to know more about Angelo and Snr Pereira and his mysterious colleague – and I'd like to know more about the business too."

"Sounds like a job for me, sir."

Burke looked at William, sitting very upright in his chair, obviously still stiff and bruised. "No, William, you are staying here and resting. Besides, I think this is more a job for Major Batarda." He turned to Juan. "Can you find out more about the set-up there? Colonel Fletcher may well be able to give you a start."

Batarda nodded. "I don't think I'll be able to answer all your questions this afternoon, but I should have made progress by tomorrow."

"Good. Let's meet up here after luncheon tomorrow. Say at three?"

"Give the poor man a break," said William. "Just because we don't take a siesta doesn't mean he can't."

Burke nodded.

"Four o'clock, then. And let's hope we can make some progress."

CHAPTER 16: Find the Frenchman!

Burke spent the next morning in the house, trying to work out what he was missing. He had wondered if he should have sent people to question other merchants so that there would be no suggestion that Snr Pereira and his business had been singled out for special attention. In the end he had decided not to. It would do no harm if Snr Pereira realised that his was the only business to be questioned in this way. Anything that made people nervous made them more likely to make mistakes – and he desperately needed somebody to make a mistake.

"We're thrashing around and getting nowhere," he complained when William joined him with a mid-morning cup of coffee. "I know I'm missing something, but I have no idea what it is."

William poured himself a cup. He didn't particularly like coffee, but he felt that beer in the middle of the morning might be frowned upon and he had a superstitious belief that drinking liquid somehow lubricated his brain.

"You've got me talking to servants and we're trying to track down these people that we saw in the tavern. I have the feeling that we're starting at the bottom of this conspiracy and trying to work our way up. Perhaps we should be working out who is at the top and tracing things downward."

"Well, the suggestion is that this whole affair is a plot by disaffected aristocrats. So we start at Morais and Carvalho and work down from them."

"But it isn't Morais and Carvalho, is it? They're just not that bright. When we saw them at *A Tendinha* did they look like the masterminds of a spy plot to you?"

Burke thought about what William had said. There was certainly something in it.

"I think you're right that they're not heading up a spy ring. But they are up to no good."

William sucked his teeth. "Word on the street is that there have been a lot of accidents of late. The odd fire. Some sort of irritant mixed in with the starch that the soldiers use on their hair."

Burke grimaced. The insistence that the infantry powder their hair with starch was one of the more inexcusable peccadillos of the British Army. Men already laden down with food, ammunition, and weapons had to carry the wretched hair powder even as it was fast going out of fashion among the upper echelons of society. The practice had been abandoned by most regiments in 1808 but the Guards held onto it. He supposed that if anyone was to suffer from itching powder on their heads, it might as well be the Guards. It could stop them from behaving as if they were so damn superior – though, realistically, Burke felt that nothing could penetrate the self-belief of the guards.

Adulterated hair powder was easy enough to dismiss, but Burke thought about the maggoty meat and the broken axles. There did seem to be a lot of minor mishaps.

"So our aristocratic friends might not be concerned with espionage at all but with these petty acts of sabotage."

William nodded. "It makes sense. This Angelo fellow puts them up to it and they just organise people to piss it the Army's beer, so to speak."

"But we know there is a real attempt to gather information about the Lines. Cristiano wasn't sabotaging anything. He was at the Great Redoubt to gather information. So who was he working for? I'm sure there are some other rich young men with no loyalty to their government and time on their hands and they are quite happy to play at espionage. But I don't see that they would be any more capable of organising a spy network than those two. Do you have any suggestions?"

"My money would be on a Froggie."

"The French were driven out, William, or had that escaped your notice?"

"But suppose they'd left somebody behind to provide intelligence after they'd gone."

It was a nice idea, but where would such a person hide? And, once hidden, how could you smoke him out? Neither James nor William could come up with any suggestions. They could only hope that

Batarda could produce something helpful when he turned up that afternoon.

* * *

At first, it seemed to Burke that Batarda had drawn a blank. He could discover nothing about Angelo's life, though he was hopeful of finding out more soon. Snr Pereira's life was more of an open book, though a book so dull it was unlikely that many people would ever finish it. He had inherited the business from his father, who had inherited it from his father who had inherited it from his. Fletcher, who had made it his business to know about all the provision merchants in Lisbon, told Batarda that the firm, though long established, had gone through a difficult period.

"During the occupation they supplied the French. When the French left, they found it difficult to replace their business."

"So they had divided loyalties at the least."

"The colonel was less worried about that and more concerned that they might go bust and fail to fulfil their contracts, but then they got a substantial injection of cash from somewhere and all was well."

"Where did the money come from?"

"Nobody seems to know. None of the banks are admitting lending them anything. It seems to have been some kind of private arrangement. A sleeping partner, or some such."

"And so we come to the mysterious colleague. I'd like to know more about this fellow."

William, who had been silently following all this, now interrupted. "What does the money have to do with anything. People like Morais are rich. They don't need money passed through a provision wholesaler."

"Money always tells a story, William. The story here is that Pereira and Son is vulnerable. Snr Pereira is the fourth generation to run this business. That has to be a source of pride to him and the suggestion that it might go bust on his watch would be deeply humiliating. Then somebody comes along and offers to solve his financial problems. I imagine that somebody could attach a lot of conditions to their investment." Suddenly he stopped and struck his forehead with his fist.

"Sweet heavens, I've been such a fool. If the French intended to leave somebody behind, that should be somebody who already knows many people across the city. And who would that be?"

William and Juan both looked blank.

"What did you just say about Colonel Fletcher?"

Batarda, frowning, seemed to be trying to remember exactly what he had said. Then the frown vanished. "That he had made it his business to know about all the provision merchants in Lisbon."

Burke nodded. "Because if you are responsible for supplying an army, you have to have good connections with all sorts of businesses."

"But," said William, "the French live off the land. They don't buy what they can steal."

"Generally that's true. But they were in Lisbon for a while and everyone says that the occupation here was not too harsh. So they must have had Commissariat officers who arranged for supplies."

"You're thinking about Snr Pereira's new colleague."

"The one whose financial assistance bailed Pereira and Son out at a time when it faced bankruptcy."

"A business," put in Juan Batarda, "that had been doing a lot of work with the French."

"So this officer stays behind when the French leave and moves in on Snr Pereira's business."

"That's that, then. We arrest this French fellow and that's the job done." William's battered features arranged themselves into a smile. "No offence, Juan, but it will be good to get out of Lisbon."

"None taken, William. But where are we going to find this gentleman so we can arrest him?"

"Well, Snr Pereira will know, won't he? We may not be able to beat information out of Morais, but Pereira won't enjoy the same protection, will he?"

"I'm not sure he does know. I wonder if Angelo is there to pass messages from this 'colleague'. He takes messages to Snr Pereira and to Morais and, presumably, any other agents the French have."

William did not let this idea get in the way of his robust approach to solving the mystery. "So we pick up this Angel fellow and beat the information out of him."

"I can see the appeal," said Burke. "but I still favour the subtle approach first. Why don't you follow Angelo and see where he leads us."

William nodded. Burke felt that William shared Batarda's enthusiasm for a lead pipe and a dark room but would settle for this for the time being.

CHAPTER 17: Another bad night for William

There was many a struggling artist who would have been thrilled to have their work garner a fraction of the interest that Marta's portraits had been getting in Lisbon. Her original sketches had, thanks to Burke's efforts, done the rounds of the city's provision merchants and travelled as far as Torres Vedras. Now her sketch of William Brown was being exhibited in taverns across Lisbon. For just as Burke had used Marta's work to track down Morais' companions in crime, so Morais was, in turn, using it to find the man who had, he was now sure, been spying on him.

The portrait of William that he had taken from the girl was his best chance of tracking the Englishman down and putting an end to whatever plots were being hatched against him. Like Burke, he dared not risk losing the only picture he had of the man Marta had called Bob, so he had had copies made. They weren't as vivid as the original, but the subject was still recognisable and by now the copies were circulating throughout Alfama. It was, Morais was confident, only a matter of time.

Morais' confidence should have been unjustified. Brown's business did not regularly take him drinking in the taverns below the castle. The servants he had been befriending enjoyed more salubrious drinking dens. Now, though, he was following Angelo and Angelo's business did take him to Alfama. William's mission meant he was there several nights a week. William followed him from one bar, where he met someone whose clothes marked him out as an aristocrat, to another where he passed money to a man whose patched jacket suggested the opposite end of the social spectrum. On some nights he met several people in different places, on others he seemed content to stay drinking alone in one place all evening. Once or twice a week he would vanish upstairs with Beatriz – one of the prettier of the tavern whores – and William would wait with a glass of wine while the other wenches demanded to know why he did not buy their services too.

William was careful and Angelo would never have known he was being followed if it weren't for the whores. The girls noticed men drinking alone: such men were their best customers after all. And it did not take long for them to notice that the solitary Englishman would wait while Angelo conducted his business with Beatriz and leave as Angelo did. One of the girls mentioned it to Beatriz and she mentioned it to Angelo on his next visit. He was a good customer after all, and it never did any harm to do a customer a favour.

The next Tuesday Angelo met Morais at *A Tendinha*. Knowing now that he was being followed, he had taken a twisting course that involved unexpected dashes through back doors and slipping down passages that were almost invisible in the dark.

"Somebody's watching out for me. An Englishman. Dark hair, civilian clothes but looks like a soldier. I want to know who it is."

Morais slid the picture across to him. "Haven't you seen this?"

He had, of course, but he had paid it little attention. He had better things to do than help Morais with his grubby concerns. He had people to sort that kind of thing out for him – Morais for one.

"Who is he?"

"We don't know, but now we can find out. If he's following you, you need only let us know where you'll be going tomorrow and we can take care of him."

Angelo looked disdainfully at Morais and the fellow who always followed him around like a bewigged poodle. How he despised them! They were not men to be trusted in a fight. He had heard about their adventure with the girl. She'd got away, hadn't she? And that was just a girl. They could hardly be trusted to deal with whoever this man was.

"Don't worry. I can handle this."

He took the paper with the sketch and rose to his feet. He was suddenly anxious to be off.

* * *

Angelo did not like the Frenchman who issued him with his orders, but he respected his cunning. Being based at Pereira and Son provided him with a ready supply of men who were far more suited to the sort of violence he had in mind than the effete dandies he had been dealing with. He despised them, but they had their uses. One day they would no longer be needed and then they would regret their superior airs.

When he left his lodgings the next night, two of the warehousemen lurked in the shadows behind him. Santiago and Duarte were not the biggest of the men he could have used, but they were the most brutal.

William might have bested them in a fair fight – or even the sort of brawl that passed for a fair fight in his life. But what happened could hardly be describes as a fight at all. One minute he was following Angelo, keeping quite close because he did not want to risk losing him again. The next he heard sudden footsteps behind him and had only time to make a half turn before something struck his head and the world turned dark.

CHAPTER 18: The slaughterhouse

He could not make out much of the room he was in. Being tied down to a table gives you a good view of the ceiling but little else. There was an animal stink, though, and the sharp, tangy smell of blood.

What he could see, all too clearly, was the face of Angelo who was bending over him and asking a question. He seemed to have been asking it for a while.

There was a sting as his face was slapped. For the first time the fog on his brain lifted enough for him to understand what he was being asked. "Who are you?"

That was easy enough. "I'm William Brown. I'm a sergeant in His Majesty's army and if you don't release me, it will go ill with you."

His answer seemed not to satisfy the clerk.

"You are not wearing a uniform."

William gave a silent sigh. He'd tried telling the truth and that had been breath wasted. He had the feeling he and Angelo were never going to be friends.

"You're not wearing a uniform, but you smell of frog."

Angelo raised a hand and one of his thugs stepped forward and passed him a long pole with a metal end. "They use this for driving the pigs towards the slaughterer." He swung the end into William's chest. It was not sharp. Clearly the idea was not kill him – at least not yet.

"So, Sergeant Brown, if you are not wearing a uniform, you must be a spy."

William said nothing and the metal smashed into his thigh. "Answer me."

"You haven't asked a question."

This time it was his forearm. He bit against the inside of his cheek. He was damned if he was going to scream.

"I'm off duty. There's no requirement I wear a uniform."

"British NCOs don't have the money to buy their own clothes. They always wear their uniforms."

"I gamble. I win at cards and I like to get out of my uniform sometimes."

His chest again. It landed on one of his cracked ribs. He bit harder on his cheek.

"Somebody bought you those clothes. Who was it?"

He said nothing but watched the pole rise. Angelo hesitated a moment, and William saw him deciding where to strike.

It was going to be a long night.

CHAPTER 19: Another rescue party

Burke woke and lay still for a moment, enjoying the silence of the early morning. Not that a house like that of Snr Lopez was ever entirely silent. He could hear the tread of one of the maids on the stairs as she prepared the downstairs rooms for the day. Faintly, in the distance, there was the clatter of cutlery as breakfast was laid out.

What there wasn't, he realised, was the sound of William Brown approaching with his morning tea.

Burke was instantly wide awake. The last time Brown had failed to make an appearance in the morning, Burke had not reacted immediately. Now, thinking of the state William had been in after his beating, he resolved that he was not going to delay again.

Ten minutes later he had checked Brown's room and established that he had not slept there.

Snr Lopez at first sought to reassure him. Surely his sergeant had simply met a friend or come by some minor accident. He took one look at Burke's face, though, and his attempts at reassurance spluttered to a halt.

"Was he on a mission for you?"

Burke nodded grimly.

"A dangerous mission?"

He had not thought it was, but now he realised he had been a fool. William's sudden disappearance had to be something to do with Angelo, which meant that finding Angelo was his first step.

There was the ringing of a bell announcing a visitor at the front door and, for a moment, Burke imagined it might be William but his relief was short lived as he heard Batarda's voice in the hall. "Any progress yet?" he asked.

"You could say that." Burke explained the situation.

"I'm going to ride over to Pereira's offices and find out where this Angelo is. Are you coming?"

Of course Batardo was coming.

Burke nodded his acknowledgement and the two men were off.

* * *

Twenty minutes later, he threw himself off his mount in Pereira's yard. Batardo stayed with the horses while Burke pushed through the crowd that always hung around the doors.

Two men were busy in the clerks' room. Neither of them was Angelo.

"Where is Angelo?"

Shrugs. Nobody knew or, if they did, they would not admit to knowing.

Burke crossed towards Snr Pereira's door. One of the clerks hurried from his stool standing in Burke's path.

"Senhor, do you have an appointment?"

"See this uniform? I don't need a bloody appointment."

The clerk held his ground, which was a mistake.

"Snr Pereira insists…"

That was as far as he got. Burke grabbed a forearm in each hand, lifted him from the ground, turned around, and pushed him none-too-gently back towards his stool.

He opened the door to the inner office to find Snr Pereira already on his feet.

"Who do you think you are to …"

He didn't wait for the man to finish.

"Where's Angelo?"

Pereira called through the open door. "Get Francisco and Afonso up here."

"I don't want Francisco and Afonso. I want Angelo."

"I have no interest in discussing the whereabouts of my staff with you. You can leave now or I will have you thrown out."

Burke's frustration with the whole situation and his fears for William drove him across the room. Pereira was leaning over his desk, almost spitting at Burke as he spoke. Burke stepped forward, grabbed a handful of his hair and pulled his head sharply down onto the desk. Pereira was clearly unused to violence and his scream was of shock as much as pain. The sight of his blood pouring profusely from his nose made Burke feel that their conversation might shortly prove more productive.

At that moment, though, the sound of booted feet running through the clerks' room signalled the arrival of two men who Burke assumed must be Francisco and Afonso. They were big men, their muscles well developed, presumably from years of loading crates of vegetables onto Pereira's carts. They had the air of men who were comfortable with violence. Burke imagined that Snr Pereira must find them useful to have around when faced with customers who were slow to pay their bills. He smiled. He felt he needed the exercise.

These men might be big and strong and their appearance alone probably terrified most of their victims into submission before much had happened in the way of violence, but they were clearly amateurs. The door was only wide enough to admit one and the first man – was it Francisco or Afonso, Burke wondered – pushed through ahead of his companion. Burke stepped sharply to one side at the doorway as his would-be assailant was carried forward by his own momentum. Burke simply stuck a foot out and tripped him. It wasn't that impressive as a fighting move but now there was one man on the floor and a second spinning round trying to avoid falling over his companion. As he turned to face Burke, Burke hit him once, very hard, in the gut.

The fall hadn't done any serious injury to the first man, who now made the mistake of trying to get to his feet. Burke stepped over his other victim and kicked him in the head.

That was that. It had hardly counted as exercise – Burke wasn't even breathing hard – but it had served to release some of his frustration. It had also had a salutary effect on Snr Pereira, who now seemed anxious to be as helpful as possible. No, he still didn't know where Angelo was but perhaps Colonel Burke had considered checking some of his firm's other properties?

Such as?

There was a shed at the docks where they stored fish fresh off the boats.

Burke considered the possibility. If William was being held there, it needed to be somewhere reasonably isolated. Was the shed isolated?

No, it was on the dockside. There were people passing it all day.

Where else?

They had a small stockyard on the edge of town. They had their own butchers and stock was slaughtered and butchered there. Yes, of course it was isolated: nobody wanted to live next to that noise and smell.

Where is it?

An address to the north.

Burke turned and left, pausing only to kick the two warehousemen on the way out. He already felt better, but he decided he needed to take any small satisfactions that the day might offer.

Batarda was waiting outside with the horses. Burke gave him the address. Did he know the place?

He nodded. "I know the area. We'll ride there and then follow the smell."

And they were off.

* * *

The rebuilding of Lisbon after the earthquake had left the city with beautiful straight wide streets. Burke and Batarda put their spurs to their horses and thundered off.

Soon they were out of the city centre and making their way rather more slowly through streets that had been there before the earthquake. Here, the maze of rutted roads had all-too-clearly grown over hundreds of years. The earthquake had made things worse as many of the smaller tracks (for that is all a lot of them were) had been blocked by falling buildings. Batarda led the way, but he had to check and change direction every few minutes. Burke knew the man was doing his best and, without his help, he could ride in circles for hours and never find the slaughterhouse. He was hard put to keep his temper, though. He was haunted by the thought of what might be happening to William and the idea that it was all, in the end, his fault.

The area that they rode through – the remains of ruined houses, the empty plots of land, the dogs lurking in the ruins – added to his sense of dread. The few men they saw around the homes that still stood looked villainous types. It was, Burke knew, unreasonable to assume that everybody living there was a fugitive or a rogue. Many were just poor. Even so, it was a neighbourhood where an honest man could not be sure of help if he was in trouble.

It was a still day, but a sudden breeze carried on it the smell of carrion.

"We're close." Batarda pointed northward. "That way, I'd say."

* * *

It was another ten minutes before they saw ahead of them the building that had to be Pereira's slaughterhouse. It was a long, low building with a fenced-off yard in front of it. The ground of the stockyard was beaten earth. It was empty, though the smell of shit and blood and terror still hung in the air.

The place might well have been deserted but Batarda pointed to a cart left propped in a corner of the yard. "There's someone here."

"It's just a cart. There's no horse."

"It's a slaughterhouse," said Batarda. "Animals are driven to the stockyard and killed. Somebody drives over from Pereira & Son, picks up the butchered corpses and takes them back to the warehouse for distribution. Why would they leave the cart here?"

"So where's the horse?"

"Taken out of harness and tucked away round the back out of sight."

"Let's take a look."

They tied the reins of their own horses to the stockyard rails and walked quietly towards the side of the building. Burke cursed their uniforms. He'd worn a red coat to impress Snr Pereira. It hadn't impressed him at all and now the two of them were trying to approach a building inconspicuously in the most conspicuous possible clothing. Still, whoever was there was not advertising their presence so with any luck they were lurking inside and had not placed sentries.

The building that faced onto the stockyard was made of wood and gave the impression of being several decades old. If it had not survived the earthquake, perhaps the owners had simply rebuilt it out of the existing wood. Big double doors led from the yard so animals could easily be driven in. A smaller door at the side presumably led to offices. A window beside the door was shuttered.

Batarda and Burke passed the shuttered window and moved towards the back of the building. Another door and, beside it, the horse.

"There can't be that many of them. Should we just kick in the door and take the bastards?"

"There are two other doors out. They could kill William and take to their heels." If William isn't dead already, he thought, and pushed the idea away. "Let's try the door quietly. It might not even be locked."

They tried the door by the horse first. The animal shifted as they approached and they froze. Might the sound of its nervous shuffling bring someone to the door to check?

Nobody came and eventually the horse settled and Burke very slowly tried the door. It was on a simple latch which lifted immediately, but when he pushed gently at the door, he felt the resistance of a bolt.

Shaking his head at Batarda, he moved back to the other small door. Again he lifted the latch and pushed, expecting again to find it locked. This time, though, it opened. It seemed that whoever was here had become careless.

They were in a small office. There was a chair, a table and pigeonholes on the wall. Batarda poked through the papers.

"Orders for meat, payments, receipts. Just what you'd expect to see really."

Burke nodded. There was only one door out of the room and now he put his ear to it and listened. Somebody – two people maybe – was talking quietly. He eased the door open. Through the crack he saw a large room. There were butchers' blocks, some with choppers and butchers' knives lying on them. Hooks hung from the ceiling. There were no carcases there but the place stank of blood. Somewhere beyond what he could see through the crack, two men were talking and now he could catch most of what they were saying.

"It's alright for Angelo. He goes and puts his head down. Poor little lamb is tired. But we don't need to rest. 'Stay here and watch him,' he says. Why can't the lazy bugger watch him himself?"

"Give it a rest, Lucio. We're getting paid, aren't we? And it's not like it's hard work. I don't think he's going anywhere, is he?"

There was a bark of laughter.

He turned to Batarda. "Two men here, Angelo somewhere else."

"How do we take them?"

"They're too far away to rush. We're going to walk in like we own the place. Let's see how impressive these uniforms really are."

He opened the door quietly and the two of them stepped through.

Once inside, they could see Lucio and his friend standing near a butcher's block at the far side of the room. Each block was like a very solidly made table with a top a good three or four inches thick. They were big enough to put a whole pig or lamb on. Burke found himself wondering, irrelevantly, how you would butcher a cow. Hang it from one of the hooks in the ceiling, he guessed, and cut it into quarters that could be fitted onto the block.

They walked side by side towards the two men. Now Burke could see that there was something on that last block, but it did not look like a pig or a lamb. Maybe it was the sight of William laid out like a slab of meat, but something made his next step a little firmer and his footsteps were suddenly loud enough to attract attention.

The windows were all shuttered, but light filtered through from grimy skylights in the ceiling. Burke saw the two men turn and stare. They would have seen two uniformed figures moving quietly towards them. There was no shouting, no threats, just the implacable advance of two men seeking vengeance.

They stared for, it seemed, two or three seconds before they reacted.

"Oi! This is private property; you can't be here."

He sounded, Burke thought, like a respectable citizen seeing off an itinerant beggar. It was almost funny, but he wasn't smiling as, without breaking step, he picked up a butcher's cleaver from the block as he walked past it. Out of the corner of his eye he saw that Batarda had already picked up a knife.

They were only three or four paces from the nearest man now. He had stepped towards them but now seemed to realise that he was unarmed and they were not. He turned back to grab up a knife of his own and Burke threw the cleaver which spun once, lazily, in the air and then landed in his back. He screamed and kept on screaming, so it seemed he wasn't dead, but Burke was fairly sure he soon would be.

The other man had grabbed up a knife but his eyes kept looking towards the twitching body of his friend. Burke moved forward at the same steady, remorseless pace. He could see William's body on the block now, tied down to the wood at his wrist and ankles. There was a lot of blood and one of his hands was at an angle to his arm that meant a broken wrist. Burke forced himself to concentrate on the immediate problem – the man with the knife. He was backing away but if Burke turned to attend to William, he would take the opportunity to attack. So, hard as it was, Burke ignored William and moved steadily toward his target.

Lying on the table beside William was a solid stick with a metal ball at the end. There was blood on the ball. Burke picked it up as he passed and hefted it experimentally in his hand. It seemed a useful weapon, particularly if he wanted his next victim left alive.

The man had retreated until his back was against the wall. Burke kept moving forward, the stick raised. Desperately the man threw himself towards Burke, knife arm outstretched. It was a particularly stupid thing to do. Burke brought the stick down and the metal ball landed on his forearm. The knife fell from his grip and Burke swung the stick again into his gut.

"Don't let him get up," he told Batarda. "I want to see to William."

Burke picked up a knife and cut the ropes tying William to the table. A moan as he cut the rope holding down the broken wrist confirmed that William was alive and more-or-less conscious.

"Hold on," said Burke. "We'll have you out of here soon. But there's still one man left to deal with and it won't be safe to move you until we've finished him."

As he spoke, he heard movement. There was another door on the side of the room which he judged must lead to the locked entrance where they had found the horse and the sounds came from the other side of that door. Leaving Juan watching their prisoner, he crossed the room to listen. He heard the sound of footsteps, the creak of a rusty hinge and then nothing.

He pushed at the door but it did not open. Another push and it barely moved.

It took a while, but eventually he got it wide enough open to see the door had been barricaded with a pile of furniture.

"He's on his heels out through the back door from the look of it."

There was no point in hurrying. Angelo would be long gone.

Batarda abandoned his prisoner just long enough to help Burke push the door open until he could squeeze through.

The room contained a couple of chairs, a table, and a camp bed, all now shoved up against the door. Angelo must have done it while they were dealing with the guards outside. There had been enough noise – screaming mainly – to have masked the scrape of the furniture.

The room must have been used when they had stock held overnight and they needed someone to stay there. Angelo, it seemed, had found torturing William so exhausting he had needed to take advantage of the bed and had decided to stay there safely out of the way once he heard the arrival of the rescue party.

The outside door was now unbolted and Burke moved from the gloom of the slaughterhouse into the bright sunlight. He looked toward the rail where the horse had been hitched. There was no horse.

Back inside, Juan had found some rope and trussed up the prisoner. He had got a mug from somewhere and was cradling William and holding water to his lips.

"We need to get him out of here," he said.

Burke nodded his agreement. "He can't be left. Angelo has taken his horse, but the cart must still be here. We should be able to harness up one of our horses and carry him home in that."

"We could take him to my mother. He needs nursing and poor Snr Lopez must be tired of his house being used as a hospital."

"He's in a bad way. Can your mother cope?"

"She has Marta to help."

There was something so disingenuous in Batarda's tone that Burke was immediately suspicious. "I suppose you'll need to check on his progress every day."

Juan at least had the decency to blush. "It would leave you free for your other duties."

Burke shrugged. He would visit William every day in any case, but he was happy to give the major an excuse to see more of Marta. The two seemed to be growing increasingly fond of each other and if they gave each other joy, at least some good would have come out of this mess.

"We'd better get one of the horses harnessed up."

"So long as the cavalry never find out that we used one of their mounts as a carthorse."

They hurried to where they had left their horses. To Burke's relief they were still there. Angelo had obviously been so panicked that he had mounted his own beast and galloped off without thinking to find their mounts and drive them away.

Not that their horses would necessarily have moved if Angelo had made the attempt. It was soon clear that, while the horses had been well trained to do everything that could reasonably be expected of a cavalry mount, they took exception to new ideas. In particular, they shared the view of their regiment that pulling carts was beneath them. One seemed less temperamental than the other, but it still took a while to get it harnessed up and ready to move. William then had to be eased gently into the cart. Their prisoner was dumped, considerably less gently, alongside him. Batarda took the reins as Burke rode alongside and kept a careful eye on their passengers.

There were no springs on the cart. Batarda drove slowly, doing his best to dodge the worst of the potholes on the road but, even so, William's battered body was punished with every jolt along the way. He never cried out or complained but Burke could see him grimace in pain as the cart bumped on its way.

Burke knew he should be hurrying in pursuit of Angelo. He had a faster horse and a fair idea of where the fugitive would have gone, but he could not leave Batarda until he knew William was safe.

It seemed to take forever, but gradually they moved out of the semi-wasteland around the slaughterhouse and found themselves riding into a more respectable suburb a mile or so from where Batarda's mother lived.

The sound of the cart rattling up to her house brought Batarda's mother to the door. "It's Juan," she called back into the house and Marta dashed out, obviously thrilled to see him there. One look at his face brought her to a halt.

"It's William," said Batarda, gesturing towards him.

The two women hurried to the cart, clucking over Brown's condition. They ignored James' attempts to take charge and issued a string of orders. Batarda was sent to lift a door off its hinges to provide a makeshift stretcher.

"Now ease him onto the door." Getting William out of the cart and into bed was not a simple task and it was accompanied with a continuous stream of commands from both of the women, who complained at the men every time their efforts brought William the slightest discomfort. Even William, who had barely made a sound on the journey ended up hissing between painfully clenched teeth, "Let them alone. They're doing their best."

Finally, he was settled in bed with the two women vying with each other in the nursing stakes, and Burke and Batarda turned back to their business.

"What are we going to do with him?" Juan nodded towards the man trussed up in the cart.

"I've got a few questions before we decide." Burke looked around. "Let's drive somewhere quieter."

Ten minutes later, Batarda found another scrap of waste land abandoned after the earthquake. It was in a little hollow with broken bricks and chunks of masonry lying on the ground but no houses within sight. Burke climbed into the cart and asked his questions.

He would have been happy to beat answers out of their prisoner, but that was not to be necessary. One look at Burke's face left the man with no illusions about what was likely to happen to him if he was not cooperative. He and Lucio both did occasional work for Pereira and Son and Angelo had asked them to help him.

"Pereira and Son seems to have a goodly number of men who enjoy a fight."

He shrugged. "It's heavy work. Pereira's employs big lads."

"And you have a side-line in violence."

Another shrug. "We're poor men, senhor. It pays the bills."

"Was this a job you did just for Angelo or did Snr Pereira know."

"Snr Pereira manages the fruit and veg. Angelo manages the rest of the work."

"The rest of the work?"

"When we need a man injured or killed. When someone is to be threatened or somebody is to be paid off: all that is organised by Angelo."

"But Angelo is only a clerk."

"Maybe. But he is not a clerk for Snr Pereira. He clerks for someone else. Someone who runs the other side of the company."

"Who is that?"

"I don't know, senhor. It is somebody who does not want to be known. That is why his instructions are always sent through Angelo. I think it might be very unhealthy to try to find out who he is."

Burke walked away with Batarda, leaving their prisoner trussed up in the cart.

"He's talking about this mysterious colleague of Snr Pereira isn't he?" said Juan.

"That seems more than likely. I think he's telling the truth and he has nothing much more to give us, but I don't think we can let him go. If this ever comes to a trial, or even some sort of formal inquiry, people are going to want to hear his evidence. In any case, he knows where your mother lives and where we've left William, so I don't fancy turning him loose to spread that information about."

Batarda looked thoughtful. "So you want somewhere where he can be safely stowed away until we want him again."

"That's about the size of it. Do you have somewhere in mind?"

"A couple of hundred somewheres. I think he could join a labour detail on one of the unfinished forts. The workers there are by way of being patriots, so they'll be happy to keep an eye on him and make sure he doesn't abscond. I'm sure Colonel Fletcher will be happy to arrange his transport up there. Until then we can chuck him in a spare stall in the colonel's stables."

It seemed that Snr Pereira and his wholesale operation wasn't the only business in town capable of running dark operations alongside their legitimate front.

"You go and sort things with Colonel Fletcher. I'm overdue an interview with Snr Pereira."

CHAPTER 20: Book-keeping

Burke arrived at Pereira and Son to discover that Angelo had been and gone which, given the lead he had, was hardly surprising. What was more surprising was that Snr Pereira seemed to have gone too. The daily business of the place was carrying on: carts continued to arrive at the warehouse; stable lads still busied themselves with the horses; the usual crowd of farmers was gathered at the office door. Inside, though, there was chaos. Pereira might have been an ineffective manager but bills still had to be paid and contracts had to be signed and after only an hour or two there was already a growing pile of papers waiting on his desk.

Burke wasted little time in the building. His birds had flown. By the time he left, though, the crowd around the doors was growing fast. There were mutterings that no payments were being made and the crowd showed every sign of turning into a mob.

There was no longer any chance of keeping his investigation quiet. The time for subtlety was over. Pereira's yard needed to be sealed off before any other people who might be involved in the plot also took to their heels. In any case, Burke could always justify closing down the yard by the need to preserve public order before Pereira's creditors started a riot.

Burke used his authority as one of Beresford's staff officers to call out a militia platoon to close the street. Beresford would complain, of course, but even the general would accept his logic eventually.

The first stones had just been thrown by farmers who saw no signs of Pereira and Son being in any position to pay them when the militia turned up. Burke had some sympathy with the farmers but he was professionally impressed with the speed at which the militia, with bayonets fixed, cleared out the yard. In fact, he had to step in to stop them clearing out the staff as well.

"Everybody who doesn't work here gets thrown out. Everybody who does, stays here."

Some warehousemen tried to slip out with the farmers and one or two may even managed, but Burke was confident that he had most of the potential conspirators trapped. He doubted that Angelo and his two thugs were the only ones on the payroll who were involved in spying for the French.

Confident that the place was sealed off, Burke returned to Pereira's office. This plot was well-financed and, as he had said to Batarda, following the money can tell you a lot.

The clerks by now had given up their frantic activity of earlier and were sitting, apparently stunned, at their desks.

Did anybody have any idea where the keys to the safe might be? No, Snr Pereira had always kept them on his person. "But, senhor," spoke up one of the older clerks, his voice quavering with nerves, "Snr Pereira did take money from the safe before he left."

No surprise there, thought Burke.

"Did he leave his account books?"

A chorus of voices assured him that the books would never have left the office.

Burke settled himself behind Snr Pereira's desk and started through the books. He was pleasantly surprised by how well ordered the accounts were. Presumably after three generations the Pereira men imbibed good practice bookkeeping with their mother's milk.

It took less than half an hour to confirm what Fletcher had already told Batarda: the business was running at a loss. Pereira might have cleaned out the safe before he fled, but he could have taken hardly any money with him. A separate ledger recorded payments to the bank but the deposits bore no relationship to the profit and loss account of the business.

Could any of the clerks explain where the money came from? Burke's question was met with blank stares. Every week one of them had been sent off to the bank with a satisfyingly heavy bag of coin and a couple of the larger warehousemen acting as bodyguards. They had always assumed that this money, like their wages, came from the profits of the business. When Burke explained that the business was not making any profit, he was met with incredulity.

The oldest of the clerks – the one who had reported Pereira's raid on the safe – joined Burke in the office to check that he was reading the accounts properly. As he did so, his face, already lined with age, showed deeper furrows on his forehead. "I don't understand. You see here…" He pointed at one line of the ledger. "That's the price we were paid for a sack of wheat sold to the army. But that's far too cheap. Look here." He pointed at another line in the ledger. "This is the price we should have been paid."

Burke compared the two sums. Fletcher was right. Even allowing that Pereira might have been giving the army a discount because of the scale of their business, the price was far too low.

Tomorrow, he decided, he would return with a bookkeeper and explore all the mysteries of Pereira and Son's economics. He locked the office, dismissed all the clerks except for the old man who had been helping him, and turned his mind to the warehouse staff.

There were a lot of warehousemen and all were, as their prisoner had said, big men. All would have to be questioned and that, like the account books, was not something for him to do on his own that afternoon. More militia men were summoned and they marched all of Snr Pereira's warehouse staff off to the castle where they could be safely imprisoned somewhere in the bowels of the keep. It was unfair, Burke knew. Many of them doubtless led blameless lives but until he knew which ones he could trust, it was safer to lock them all up.

There were many things Burke disliked about his nefarious trade as a confidential agent of the King. He often envied those officers who wore their uniforms proudly and who were strangers to the dark doings that were his everyday business. What he did not envy them, though, was the administrative chores of office – chores that he was usually able to bypass. Today, though, was going to be a day for writing requests, issuing orders, placing guards, and placating the civil authorities who were, understandably, wondering why the militia had been called out to guard a warehouse in the town. He even had to arrange accommodation for his prisoners. Surely, he thought, there was more than enough cellar space in the castle, but no: if you wanted twenty men locked away you needed to fill out billets, arrange for food and even argue with the castle authorities (all Portuguese and therefore not answerable to him) about who was going to pay for it all. Beresford, he knew, was not going to like this at all.

At least the evening was to prove more convivial. Snr Lopez had invited Batarda to join them for dinner. The merchant had heard of the excitement at Pereira and Son. "It's big news in our little world. All the merchants of Lisbon are agog to know what has been happening. I'm hoping that you and Major Batarda will between you be terribly indiscreet and tell me all about it."

Relaxing over a roast chicken dinner washed down with a *tinto douro*, Burke was happy to outline what they had discovered at Pereira and Son. "We'll know a lot more once we've got an expert to look through their books."

Lopez gestured so enthusiastically that the wine he was holding threatened to spill out of its glass. "But you have an expert. I don't supply food, but I have been a merchant here my whole life and I deal with the British too. If Pereira's books have a secret to tell, I am sure I will be able to find it out."

"And I can help," chimed in Batarda. "I'm happy to assist Snr Lopez in the office."

"Aren't you supposed to be finding out more about the man that ran the commissariat for the French?"

Batarda raised his hands with an apologetic shrug. "I have asked everyone I can but nobody in the castle now can help at all. The French had fled by the time the British arrived, so none of Marshal Beresford's men had any dealings with them. There may be some of our own people who knew him, but no-one is going to want to admit that they had had dealings with the French."

"Oh, for heaven's sake!"

Burke turned in surprise to their host, who was visibly agitated.

"Did it never occur to you to ask me?"

"You knew him?"

"Not personally, no. But I sold things to the French. They were good customers. The fighting was over. Life continued. Of course everyone in business dealt with the French. It doesn't mean we liked them."

"So you know who we are looking for?"

"Quite possibly. Are you looking for Colonel Moulin, who ran the commissariat, or the officers who dealt with merchants in Lisbon?"

"Did Moulin not deal with merchants himself?"

"Oh, good heavens, no. He was far too grand. In fairness, administering the Commissariat is pretty much a full time job. He had a couple of majors who were responsible for negotiating deals on the ground. I dealt with Major Garnier. He was responsible for non-food items. Not so much actual military stuff – that was sent from France – but furniture and stationery: all the home comforts the officers wanted for a long stay in Lisbon."

"What about food?"

"That would have been Major Laurent. I didn't have any business with him myself, but I met him socially once or twice with Major Garnier. Interesting man, Garnier. Used to be in the cavalry but invalided out with a gammy leg after Austerlitz and moved to the Commissariat. He must have found it very dull. I think he hankered to get back into action somehow."

The maid came in to clear the plates and returned with a cheese board. Conversation lagged as everyone helped themselves to cheese. During the pause, Burke worried at what Lopez had said. There was something there, if he could only think of it.

"Does anybody know where Garnier went when the French pulled out?"

Lopez shrugged.

"Why would anybody know?" asked Batarda. "The French withdrew in reasonably good order but they hardly left us forwarding addresses. He'll be somewhere in Spain, I imagine."

Burke shook his head, as if hoping to shake out some detail he was not yet able to place. "There's something that Snr Lopez said. This Garnier sounds the sort of person we might be looking for. But where would he hide himself away in Lisbon?"

There were more shrugs, more shaking of heads and the three of them agreed that they had no idea. If Garnier was the man they wanted, he could be anywhere.

* * *

Burke had often wondered what it would be like to be a colonel and have others do all the work for you. Now he was finding out and it wasn't as enjoyable as he had thought it would be.

Lopez and Batarda settled into Pereira's office and started on a systematic examination of his books while, up in the castle, the interrogation of the prisoners was under way. Burke found himself shuttling between the two, trying to put together the pieces of the puzzle. Wherever he was, there seemed to be other people better at the work than he was.

Snr Lopez was polite but firm. "I've been running a business all my life. I can read accounts the way that you would read – well, whatever it is you read."

The gaolers in the castle were equally firm, if not as polite. "Marshal Beresford was very clear. No British officer can abuse a Portuguese prisoner. Fortunately, we are Portuguese and can do whatever we want." They obviously shared William's enthusiasm for a robust approach to interrogation.

Both the gaolers and the bookkeepers promised results soon.

The only good news was that Pereira had turned up. Burke had both the militia and the civil authorities watch for the man and now they had found him. The bad news, though, was that he was dead.

It took a while for the word to reach Burke as the messenger had struggled to catch him shuttling between one place and another.

"Some fishermen pulled the body out of the harbour," he was told. Was it suicide or could it have been an accident? That seemed unlikely, the messenger had replied laconically. "They say his throat was cut."

Angelo tidying up loose ends, Burke thought.

He had little that needed doing that afternoon and a trip to visit Pereira's widow seemed at least a courtesy and might provide some insight as to how Pereira had got caught up in espionage. At least it would get him away from both the castle and Pereira's office.

Pereira lived in a fine house in the new quarter of Lisbon. It was far from the most expensive area, but Burke could see how Pereira might easily have found himself in financial trouble. The news of the wholesaler's death had arrived ahead of him and the door knocker was wreathed in black crepe.

There were no mourners there to comfort the grieving widow. Was it that the news had yet to spread or was Pereira not a popular man?

Sra Pereira looked to be about thirty years old. She might usually, Burke thought, be beautiful but her face was etched with care. Burke couldn't help but feel that she seemed more worried than grief-stricken, but then she I had every reason to fear for the future. Her son, around ten years old, Burke thought, sat quietly beside her. So this was the boy that should one day have taken his place alongside his father in Pereira and Son. Was it for the child that Pereira had betrayed his country?

Burke muttered the conventional words of sympathy to Sra Pereira and she bowed her head and (with some effort, Burke thought) squeezed out a tear.

"It was a terrible way to die, senhora. We think it may have been one of his workers."

"Angelo," she said, without prompting. "I only met him once. He was an unpleasant man. My husband feared and loathed him."

"And yet he was one of his chief clerks."

"He had some hold over my husband, I think, but I don't know what."

"And you have no idea where this Angelo might be now?"

"No." She was half whispering. "No idea." She lifted her face to his and he saw pride and anger flare up briefly. "My husband was not a bad man, whatever people say. He worked hard and provided for his family. The war has not been kind to us. Perhaps he was weak, but he was not a bad man." And then her head sank again and Burke felt the interview to be at an end.

Burke rode slowly back to Snr Lopez's house. Pereira's death had given him no pleasure, but at least it meant that he had something positive to report to General Beresford. (He could not think of him as Marshal Beresford: the Portuguese rank was just too absurd.) Back in his room he wrote a letter requesting a meeting and despatched a servant to carry it to the British headquarters. Barely half an hour after the message had been delivered a cavalry trooper brought a reply. General Beresford would see him at eight o'clock the following morning.

Burke did not look forward to the meeting.

* * *

He arrived at the anteroom to the commander's office expecting to spend a while with Beresford's clerk but instead found himself whisked in to face the general.

Beresford looked hot and irritated. That was, Burke felt, his natural state. He was kept standing while Beresford complained about him deploying the militia on his own authority. Much was said about protocol and even more about costs. Then, having apparently satisfied some primal need to give Burke a hard time, he gestured to a seat and, as if he had not been berating him only a minute earlier, asked, "So, Burke, are you going to tell me what the hell has been going on?"

His tone was almost avuncular – or at least as avuncular Burke could imagine him capable of – and he decided to tell him the whole story. Well, almost the whole story: it was sufficient to say that the French were engaged in spying without mentioning the Lines. What Beresford didn't know, he couldn't let slip to anyone else. Colonel Fletcher's secret was still safe.

Beresford listened without interrupting, scratching the odd note when names were mentioned. Burke finished with an account of the previous day's excitement and the measures that he was taking to progress his investigation.

When he was finished Beresford called for his clerk. "Draft me an arrest order for …" He glanced at his notes. "Snr Morais and Snr Carvalho. Lt Peterson is to take a dozen men and a closed carriage. I want it done quickly and I want it done quietly and I want the two gentlemen safely locked away in a British guard room."

This was a different side of Beresford and, for the first time, Burke could begin to see why Wellington was said to value his ability.

"You should have seized them yourself yesterday."

He was right, of course, but it was his orders that nothing must be done to upset relations with the Portuguese aristocracy that had made Burke hold back. The unfairness of the criticism stung but, before Burke could respond, Beresford continued: "Not entirely your fault after the instructions I gave, but things have gone too far to ignore what is, after all, treason."

That was, Burke thought, dangerously close to an apology. He was so shocked that he could think of nothing to say. Instead, he bowed his head in acknowledgement with a muttered, "Yes, sir."

It was the right response.

"Well done, Burke. Best be about your business. Keep me informed." And, with an uncharacteristic smile, Beresford dismissed him.

* * *

As the castle was closer than Pereira and Son, it seemed best to start by returning there.

He made his way through the twisting passageway that protected the main gate. There had been a castle here for hundreds of years and some of the cellars, he knew, went back to Roman times. He wouldn't know a Roman cellar from any other sort, but the engineering feats of the Romans fascinated Fletcher and he had told Burke about the castle's history. It had grown enormously since first the Romans and then the Arabs had started building. Now it was a maze – one that had to be navigated with care, both in terms of its geography and the politics of the place. Parts were under the control of the British who maintained a small garrison there, while most was proudly and fiercely Portuguese. The militia – Portuguese, obviously – had handed their prisoners over to their compatriots. Burke smiled at the Portuguese guard on the gate and was directed to a second guard post where he waited to be escorted to where he had left the castle gaoler the day before.

The gaoler was a large man but did not have the look of a thug. As they shook hands, Burke detected an air of weariness. He suspected that the gaoler was not entirely happy in his work.

"Most of them are innocent, you know."

Burke remembered his time impersonating a Catholic priest and taking confession over the border in Spain. "Nobody is entirely innocent, senhor."

The gaoler raised his eyes. They were brown and Burke was irresistibly reminded of the lugubrious look of a Great Dane. His voice, deep and slow, sounded much as he imagined a Great Dane would sound if Great Danes could talk. "A philosopher. Well, Mr Philosopher, I wonder how you would feel if you had spent much of the night beating a score of men who have never betrayed their country in order to find half a dozen who have."

"I've done my fair share of dirty business, senhor. It has to be justified by its results. What results do you have for me?"

The gaoler raised those sad eyes to his and then got to his feet and started out of the room, beckoning Burke to follow. They walked down a flight of stone stairs, the treads worn with the traces of thousands of feet that had climbed down them over hundreds of years.

Burke felt as if they had travelled far below ground but, when they stepped off the stairs to emerge into a corridor, light penetrated through gratings high in the walls. The gaoler pushed open a heavy door to reveal a bare cell. Again there was some light from barred windows above his head. It was enough to be able to see the six men lying on the stone flags of the floor or sat hunched against the wall. Even in the gloom, broken noses and black eyes gave evidence of their beatings. Burke was sure there was more damage under their clothing.

It was easier not to think about it. His concern was with the information that had been extracted – not the way it had been obtained.

The beatings had worked. The victims were all happy to confess that they had been working for the French. There had been occasional acts of espionage but usually nothing more serious than reporting what they had learned from porters in other firms about the quantity of supplies ordered and where they were being delivered. It was the minutiae of spying, the unconsidered trifles of intelligence that, meaningless in themselves, could be fitted together to allow a master spy to judge what units were being sent where and which were to be stood down and which were preparing for action. But as to who this master spy was, they had no idea. Their orders came always through Angelo and their information was passed back the same way. And with Angelo vanished, there was no way to find the man he reported to.

When it came to the Portuguese aristocrats happily betraying their country, most of the prisoners were unhelpful. Burke was confident that this was not because of an unwillingness to cooperate – the broken men in the cell were clearly anxious to tell all that they knew. It seemed, though, that few of Pereira's thugs had had any reason to meet these traitors. Two, though, had and were, it seemed to Burke, anxious to prove their good faith by betraying them. They did not know names, but they met these anonymous aristos in taverns: always the same taverns on the same evenings. "We knew who to speak to because there were few aristos in such places and we would always start by saying that somebody had told us they might have work for us and they would reply that they might have something in three weeks and we should talk about the possibility and then we would know they were the right people."

"But you never asked their names?"

"No, senhor. We never knew their names, nor they ours. Angelo said this kept us all safer."

Angelo, Burke thought, was right. No matter – with the names of the taverns and the days that they could expect the traitors to be there, it would be simple enough to pick them up. It was progress, he supposed. The web of spies could be broken up, but the spider at the centre was going to escape.

* * *

Back at Pereira and Son, another piece of the jigsaw was fitting into place. Snr Lopez produced another set of accounts.

"Whatever his other failings in business, old Pereira was an excellent bookkeeper," he said. He kept details of everything but scattered in separate ledgers so it takes a while to put the whole thing together. Here, you see..." He pointed at a line in the ledger. "'Payment received from Banq.' But who is Banq? The obvious suggestion is the bank, 'banco', either misspelled or a little joke by Snr Pereira – though he doesn't really seem the humorous type. But then I find a separate ledger for 'banquete'. It seems that Pereira and Son also ran a banqueting operation. It makes sense. They can provide all the food at wholesale prices and they have staff for transporting stuff there and they can hire waiters. But it's not a big business. Most of the people in this town who give large parties will have their own staff. Indeed, there's competition between the grand houses for the best chefs. So the main customer for Pereira and Son is ..." He paused like an orator waiting for applause. Then, when Burke didn't respond he said, triumphantly, "Marshal Beresford."

Burke thought back to the dinners Beresford had invited him to. They had certainly been splendid affairs, clearly served by professional waiters rather than British soldiers lured by the prospect of feeding on the leftovers and supervised by NCOs with suspicious eyes.

"Did Pereira make any money on these dinners?" asked Burke.

"Well not all the dinners were for the British administration. Hence the payment received and showing up here." He gestured toward the first entry he had drawn Burke's attention to. "But looking at these books…" – this time he gestured towards another ledger, which Burke assumed held the accounts for the banqueting business – "he seems to have been happy to take a loss when he was dealing with the British."

"Could it have been a business decision?"

Batarda, who had been listening to this exchange, snorted in derision. Snr Lopez's response was more judicious. "I suppose it's possible that Snr Pereira felt it was a useful connection to have, but it's difficult to justify this sort of loss over quite a long time."

"So it's likely that the main purpose of the banqueting business was to have access to Beresford's headquarters and the chance to eavesdrop at his dinners."

Snr Lopez nodded. Batarda grinned.

"Would you like me to pick up the banqueting staff or will you arrange it with the British?"

Burke sighed. It looked like more work for the castle's gaolers. He wished he shared the general enthusiasm for robust interrogation techniques.

"Do we have them here?"

Lopez shook his head. "No. But we are again indebted to Snr Pereira's excellent record keeping. He had details of everybody who was ever paid to work at one of these banquets," and he held up a sheet of paper covered in what Burke could see, even from across the desk, was a list of names and addresses.

"Give it to Major Batarda. He'll arrange what needs to be done."

Juan reached for the list. "Cheer up, James. You've broken up an elaborate spying operation. There was far more going on here than a few disaffected aristocrats telling tales to the French. You should be pleased." He threw up his hand in an ironic salute and set off to gather some militia men to make his arrests.

Lopez gathered some more papers from the shelves, but before he started on them, he glanced up at Burke. "Don't look so glum, colonel. Major Batarda is right. You have achieved a lot. You should be proud and happy."

Burke waved away the compliment as if he was swatting away a fly. "We've rounded up a lot of poor fools who will have confessions beaten out of them and will be lucky if they are left to rot in some cell rather than just being hanged. But the mastermind behind all this has got clear away. He's probably crossed into Spain by now." He looked around the office at the ledgers and records – all the details of Pereira's business. "Is there nothing in here that gives some clue as to who was funding all this?"

"I still suspect Major Garnier."

"That's as may be, but the name without any indication of where he is doesn't help us at all."

"I'll keep looking but, James, you need to rest. It's been a long day and you are no use to anyone in the state you're in. Go home and rest. We will meet for dinner and if I have found anything by then, I will certainly let you know."

Burke was going to object but he suddenly realised how tired he was and nodded. Lopez knew what he was doing with Pereira's records and needed no help. In fact, Burke suspected that by now he was getting in the way. Batarda was on his way to round up the latest suspects and the militia needed no help from a British colonel. The best thing he could do was to rest ready to continue the search once Lopez and Batarda had brought him more information.

He made his way out into the courtyard. The bustle that had characterised the place only a couple of days ago was gone. The warehousemen – even those whose innocence was now accepted – had abandoned Pereira and Son. The business was doomed. No carts moved across the yard; no farmers waited for payments they now knew would never come. There were still some stable lads looking after the horses owned by the firm. Burke imagined that the horses would probably be seized by the government and the stable lads would join the unemployed. Perhaps they would end up digging ditches round the forts on the Lines of Torres Vedras. He looked out for the head groom, but there was no sign of him. Perhaps he had fled the wreckage already. He, at least, should find more work. There was always employment for a man who could run a stable yard.

The death of a once thriving business – even a business that had be subsidised by French gold – was a depressing sight and Burke's mood became even darker. He unhitched his horse, which was shifting restlessly in the yard outside the office, and set off. The sooner he was home, the better.

* * *

A change of clothes – he had been in his uniform all day – improved his mood, and by the time he joined Juan Batarda and Snr Lopez for pre-dinner *petiscos* he was feeling much more human.

He asked Batarda about his day. The major was happy to oblige with an account of the various misadventures that had befallen the militia as they picked up the banqueting staff. One had dived through his window and had been followed out by an enthusiastic soldier who discovered that the fugitive had a very large dog in the yard below his rooms. "We got the fellow in the end but our poor hero had a chunk taken out of his backside and he won't be able to sit down for several days." Another had been in bed ("not with his wife," Batarda noted) and the young woman had grabbed the crucifix from the wall and started beating the militia with it. "Have you ever been attacked by a naked young woman using the image of our Lord as a deadly weapon? No one knew where to look."

It had obviously been an afternoon full of incident, but Batarda was able to report that by now everyone on Snr Pereira's list had been accounted for.

Batarda turned to Snr Lopez. "And how was your day after I left?"

"Dull compared to yours. Dull compared to anybody's, truth be told. Snr Pereira's books are dry as dust – every column neatly totalled and every cross reference filed. His is the most carefully documented tale of treachery you could wish for. I have found only one discrepancy in everything I've looked at to date."

"What's that?" asked Burke. Discrepancies were often the key to intelligence work.

"Oh, it's nothing. Just that he records income from every part of the property he owns: rental on warehousing – which he carefully debits from the mark-up on the food he stores there; wagon hire – he charges his suppliers if he picks up from their farms; rent on accommodation he provides to his workers. Everything. The Pereiras have owned that firm for three generations and they've learned how to squeeze every penny out of it. But I can't find the rent for the stable foreman's rooms. I guess he must have included it in the accounts for the stabling, but it's odd. I've seen the place from outside and it looks like prime accommodation."

Burke looked at Batarda and Batarda returned the look.

"The stable foreman with the limp," said Burke.

"The one who is really good with horses and men," said Batarda.

Both spoke together. "Garnier!"

CHAPTER 21: The chase

There was, as far as Burke was concerned, no question of dinner. Every hour, more of Pereira's men were leaving, some to go to new jobs in Lisbon, some to return to families outside the city. He would not take the risk of Garnier slipping away.

"I didn't see him when I was there," he said. "He could have left already."

"I noticed him at lunchtime." Batarda was reassuring. "We are probably in time."

"I'm sure you're in time, gentlemen. Let's eat first and do what you have to do rested and with full stomachs."

No, Burke said, they must leave now – or as soon as he had changed back into his uniform. "I'm not going to have any arguments about my authority. When I catch the bugger, I'm hauling him off into British custody." As he spoke, he was already heading for his room.

He was back in five minutes, his uniform immaculate. He was wearing his sword which he usually neglected about his daily business as it simply got in the way of normal life. Today, though, he was anxious to try it against Garnier's throat.

Batarda, as a guest, had arrived in uniform. He was glorying in his new status as a cavalry officer and wore his blue coat with its generous gold braiding on every possible opportunity. To Burke's surprise, Snr Lopez had changed too, sporting riding boots and a coat.

"I don't think you need to join us, senhor."

"Nonsense, colonel. If it's thanks to me that you've tracked this fellow down, I couldn't miss the end of the affair."

It was clear that there was no shaking him, so the three men set off together to Pereira's business. The place was almost deserted at that hour of the evening. There were a couple of militia men on the gate, protecting the premises while the authorities decided what they were going to do with them. One of them hurried inside to get their officer.

The lieutenant arrived dabbing food from his lips. He had obviously been interrupted at his dinner, but, at the sight of two officers, he pulled himself to attention.

Batarda rapped out: "The stable foreman – where is he?"

He'd left, stammered the lieutenant. There had been no orders to stop him. He had taken a cart and one of the horses.

"You let him take state property?"

He had been in charge of the stables. It seemed reasonable… The poor man ground to a halt.

Burke interrupted. "I'm sure you did your best. What time was this?"

It was four hours ago.

"And where did he go?"

"He said he had a cousin in Porto, colonel. He said he was going there."

So he was heading north: probably not to Porto but still north towards the area controlled by the French. That meant, Burke thought, probably by the road to Sintra, the road they had taken to Torres Vedras or following the line of the Tagus. Of course, there were other roads Garnier could have chosen but they had no time to lose and between them they could cover only two. Burke cursed that they did not have Sgt Brown with them, which would have enabled them to cover at least one other possible route, but Brown was still barely able to walk, let alone ride. He would have to make do with what he had got.

"Juan, you take the road to Sintra. I'll head for Torres Vedras."

"And where, colonel, do I go?"

Burke turned to Snr Lopez. "You go home, senhor."

Lopez drew himself up. "You are my guest, senhor. I have helped you so far in this enterprise and I would like to be, as I think you English say, 'in at the kill'. Please do me the honour of allowing me to assist you."

"It could be dangerous, senhor. Garnier will be a desperate man and one who has seen combat."

"I am no coward, Colonel Burke."

Burke raised his palms in surrender. It was probably a fool's errand in any case. "You had best ride with me, senhor."

Pausing only to get a description of the horse and cart ("Just a cart, colonel, and a brown gelding,") they rode out of the gate to head north. "Give it until midnight," Burke told Batarda. "If you haven't caught him by then, he's got away."

If he's abandoned the cart, Burke thought, he'll have got away anyhow. But the French had become so used to looting the countries they invaded that he supposed it may have become almost instinctive, especially for a man who had served in the Commissariat. He pushed his horse to a canter and headed north. Beside him, Snr Lopez kept pace easily.

"There's an inn on the road about an hour north of the town," he said. "In times of trouble the city gates used to be closed at night, so there was money to be made from those who found themselves locked out."

"And nowadays?"

"It's a pleasant ride for a man who wants air and a quiet place to meet another man's wife." And then, his voice more serious, "And if the French march south, we will have times of trouble again and the city may be closed at night."

"I suspect it's too near the city. Garnier will want to get a few miles behind him before he stops."

Lopez did not reply and for a while the two men rode in silence, their horses eating up the miles.

They paused when they got to the inn, but there was no sign of a cart. There was a brown horse, but it was a broken-down creature and Burke could not imagine that Garnier had chosen it.

It was, Lopez said, several hours to the next inn. Burke decided they would ride that far and, if they did not find Garnier, stay the night there and return to Lisbon the next morning.

The light was fading by now, but they were able to keep up a good pace in the dusk.

They had been riding for three hours or more when Burke imagined he saw a shape around half a mile ahead of them. They reined in their horses and stood motionless and silent. Yes, he could hear the creaking of a cart in the distance and, faintly, the sound of hoofs on the road ahead.

Both men put their heels to their horses. The chase was coming to an end and they moved from canter to gallop.

As they closed on their quarry, they heard the crack of a whip and saw the cart sway as it picked up speed. The end of the chase, though, was a foregone conclusion. True, their horses were tired, but both men were riding fine beasts and they had not been pulling a cart all the way from Lisbon.

Soon, even by moonlight, Burke could recognise Garnier as the old cavalryman turned towards him. Too late, he saw the moon glint on the carbine that Garnier drew from below his cloak. There was the crack of a shot and the spurt of flame from the muzzle was bright in the darkness. Burke felt a sting in his arm and looked down to see a tear in his sleeve. The ball had grazed him but it seemed to have no force behind it. His horse, though, whinnied and plunged forward and Burke could make out blood on the side of its neck. The ball, it seemed, had struck the horse first and then the rider, but had done no serious harm to either.

Harmed or not, the horse shied. As a cavalry mount, its instinct when it heard gunfire was to gallop forward and now it stretched its neck out and flew towards an enemy that it assumed was somewhere in the darkness ahead. Burke reined it in and forced it to turn. The cart was a hundred yards or more behind them now. Snr Lopez had caught up, riding alongside Garnier who raised his carbine. It was an empty threat, though. The weapon was empty and it was clear that Lopez knew it was no danger.

At first Burke could not believe what he was seeing. It was surely shadows and confusion in the moonlight. But, no, Lopez was definitely swinging himself from his horse and throwing himself into the waggon. Burke kicked his mount forward, hoping against hope that he would be in time to save Lopez from a violent end at Garnier's hands. But now he saw Lopez strike towards the Frenchman and it was Garnier who went down.

With nobody at the reins, the cart swung wildly from one side of the road to the other. After a few seconds, the near-inevitable happened. One wheel caught in a ditch alongside the road, the cart tilted crazily and there was the crack of an axle breaking. The horse reared in its traces but the cart wasn't going anywhere.

Lopez seemed to have seen the danger in the nick of time and had managed to hang on as the cart crashed to a halt. Garnier, though, had not stood a chance. Burke saw him fly from the wreckage, crashing head-first onto the road.

By the time he had dismounted next to the Frenchman, Lopez was already cradling the man's head. "He's still alive," he said.

"And, more importantly, so are you. What did you think you were doing?"

Lopez grinned, his teeth showing white in the moonlight. "I was not always a middle-aged merchant," he said. "I fought my way up to where I am today. It was refreshing to remind myself of the adventures of my youth."

A groan from Garnier had Burke examining him as best he could in the darkness. He was bleeding from the head but the wound did not seem mortal. One arm hung at an unnatural angle and Burke thought there might be other broken bones, but he was satisfied his prisoner would not die.

Garnier groaned again. He opened his eyes and fixed them on Burke.

"So you finally tracked me down." His voice dripped contempt. "And I was under your nose all the time."

"But your agents are being rounded up, your network has been destroyed and you, sir, are my prisoner. And soon you will tell me all you know about the way that France's spies communicate across Portugal."

"You are overconfident, young man." Garnier coughed and turned his head to one side to spit onto the ground. Turning back he reached a hand towards his pocket.

Burke grabbed his wrist. "Have a care, sir."

"I'm reaching for my snuff box. I take it that is permitted."

Burke reached into the pocket and withdrew a round snuff box. He ran his finger across the lid. It was horn, with an image pressed into it. Curious he held it up to catch the moonlight but it was too dark to make it out.

"It depicts the storming of the Bastille," said Garnier. "A great day for my country."

"A day that has led to nothing but war and tyranny. But I would not deny you your snuff whatever container you keep it in."

Garnier opened the lid and dipped in two fingers and a thumb as if to take a generous pinch.

He raised his hand towards his face and for a moment the moonlight shone not on the dark brown of tobacco, but on a white pastille which Garnier dropped into his mouth and swallowed.

Burke reached to force open Garnier's mouth but the Frenchman clenched his jaws together. Burke pinched his nose but when he was eventually forced to breathe through his mouth, he still kept his jaws closed, breathing through his teeth.

It was Lopez who stopped him. "There's no point, James. If you get your hand into his mouth he will bite you. You will never be able to force your fingers down his throat. Whatever he has swallowed is going to stay there."

Garnier smiled. "It was hemlock," he said. "If it was good enough for Socrates, it will be good enough for me. It takes a while to die, but they say it is painless and there is no antidote. If you took me back to Lisbon, I would be tortured for the information you hope to get out of me, and then I would be hanged as a spy. This is not what most people think of as a soldier's death, but it is infinitely preferable to the alternative."

"I can't force you to vomit, but you could put your fingers down your throat and save yourself. If you do, I can promise you, as an officer of His Majesty, you will not be tortured."

"But I will still be hanged. There is nothing you can do to prevent that."

Burke silently shook his head. "It's possible you might be reprieved, but I cannot promise it."

"Then this is the best way."

Lopez gestured into the darkness ahead of them. "It can't be that far to the inn. Can we get him onto a horse? He shouldn't die here, lying beside the road."

Burke looked at Garnier, who shook his head. "I have a broken arm, cracked ribs, and there seems to be something wrong with my hip. I'm in no condition to ride. But I thank you for your concern. You need not worry about me, though. I'm quite content to die here. I have seen enough good men on the field of battle die where they fell. I have served my country as a spy and, I think, as a good one. But I was always happiest as a soldier and I will die as a soldier."

"See if you can find the inn and get some sort of transport sent back here. I'll stay here with him."

Lopez's horse – a well-trained beast – had stopped after the excitement of the chase and waited patiently for his master to remount. "I'll be back as soon as I can."

Burke watched him head off into the night before turning his attention back to Garnier. It had all been a game until now, hunting down the evil French master spy. And on the way they had found real villains like Morais and Carvalho. But now he was faced with the reality of the enemy spy and what he saw was a man very like himself.

"Can I do anything for you?"

"There were some blankets in the cart."

Burke found the blankets in the wreckage and carried them to Garnier.

"There should be a bottle of brandy too."

There were several broken wine bottles but the brandy had somehow survived the crash.

He sat alongside Garnier and the two of them shared the brandy, drinking from the bottle.

"This brandy deserves better," said the Frenchman. "A proper glass and warming to a decent temperature. But if I don't drink it now, I never will.

Burke raised the bottle. "*Santé*!" he said.

"Hardly." Garnier smiled without malice.

"What should we drink to then?"

"To battles lost and battles won."

So they drank and swapped stories of the wars and the fighting they had seen. Garnier had seen more battles than Burke but they had all been in Europe and he was fascinated by the tales of war in the West Indies and South America.

"And you were in Egypt?"

"I was. And I saw your Emperor there, although, of course, he was not an emperor in those days."

"But you saw him? You saw Napoleon."

"I did, though only through a telescope at a safe distance."

"I have seen him, though, like you, only from a distance when he was addressing his troops. It was the great honour of my life."

"I can't imagine feeling like that about Wellington."

"But Wellington is just a general with some small facility for battle. Napoleon is the most remarkable man of our age. He is more than a general. He is a genius."

Burke raised the bottle. "To great generals." he took a swig and passed it across to Garnier.

"To great generals." The Frenchman drank.

They sat for a while then in silence. Finally, Burke spoke. "Look at us the two of us. Drinking to great generals and dreaming of martial glory. And in reality, we are both in the inglorious business of spying."

"It has to be done, though. Those great generals can only win their battles if they know the likely disposition of the enemy."

"But why draw in those Portuguese aristos? They can't have given you any decent intelligence, but we are rounding them up already. Their lives are wrecked and for no good reason."

Garnier started to shrug but winced in pain and the gesture stopped. Burke imagined that Garnier's expression showed a trace of self-disgust.

"They were, I know, young and stupid and I used their stupidity against them. But my work, like yours, I imagine, has its political, as well as its strictly military side. It was my job to draw them closer to France."

"By making them put itching powder in the starch for the Guards' hair?"

Garnier grinned. "That was amusing, I thought." When Burke did not respond, he added, more seriously, "Every little act of sabotage drew them closer to our cause. It made them feel important – as if they were doing something useful. They live very empty lives, you know."

Burke found himself nodding. Perhaps if Beresford had been more sympathetic to the likes of Morais and Carvalho they might not have been so easily won over to the French.

"But what about Angelo. Did you not despise him?"

Garnier sighed. "He was a thug and a villain, but he was valuable to me. I could see him around the yard and give him his orders and nobody thought anything of it. Pereira knew who I was, of course. I owned him – paid for with honest French gold. But we were never seen together. All my instructions were relayed through Angelo. It worked well." Burke saw him smile in the moonlight. "It fooled you, anyway."

"Did you know he's killed Pereira?"

"No." He started to shake his head but Burke heard a hiss of pain and Garnier was still again. "It doesn't surprise me, though. He's a callous bastard."

"Where is he now?"

Garnier took another swig of brandy. "Why should I tell you?"

"Why not? You despise him. He deserves to die and he cannot harm your cause now."

"You sound as if you have your own reasons for hating him."

"I do."

Burke told him what he had done to William Brown.

When he had finished, Garnier was silent for a while. Then: "He had no real friends but there was a whore – Beatriz, I think. She might know."

Burke grasped his hand and they sat in silence again.

Half an hour had passed and there was still no sign of Lopez. Garnier started to shiver.

"Do you want me to try to make a fire?" Burke looked at the shattered carriage. "We have plenty of wood."

"I don't think a fire will help. The hemlock is beginning to do its work. I can't feel my limbs."

Burke began to rub at Garnier's arms and legs.

"I doubt that will do any good. I can't feel you, in any case."

Where the hell was Lopez?

Burke took Garnier in his arms, holding him as he would a child. Soon the Frenchman was trembling and shortly after that came convulsions.

When Lopez eventually arrived with a carriage from the inn, he found Burke lying on the ground holding a corpse in his arms.

CHAPTER 22: Unfinished business

When Burke explained his problem to Colonel Fletcher, the Engineer was again happy to make his men available to help Burke in his search for Beatriz. They were enthusiastic about the exercise as their task was to go out on the town until they found a girl called Beatriz whose favours were available for hire. Nobody enquired as to exactly how they conducted their research and none of the soldiers cared to volunteer the information, but a Beatriz was tracked down only a few days after Garnier's death.

"She works at a tavern near the castle" explained Corporal Johnson, who was the first to claim the finder's fee that Burke had offered. "It's popular with soldiers – ours and theirs." He meant the Portuguese, of course, but at least he said it without malice. When Burke thought how much the British fighting man despised the Spanish soldiery that marched alongside them, Johnson's reference to the Portuguese seemed almost affectionate.

"There's pillow talk, I suppose."

Like all Fletcher's men, Johnson understood the importance of security. "I imagine there is, but I doubt that the men who frequent that place know much that they can give away."

Burke hoped not, but they will have known something and, whatever they knew, he suspected that by now Angelo knew it too.

"Funny thing," said Johnson. "They say she was a looker, but she's been through the wars lately. She had a black eye and a couple of missing teeth when I saw her."

"She should be pickier in her gentleman friends." Burke was confident now that Angelo was still in Lisbon and probably hiding out with Beatriz. He will have been angry and frightened and he enjoyed inflicting pain. Beatriz was lucky still to be alive.

"I don't suppose you know where she lives?"

"No, but me and a couple of the lads should be able to follow her home. If she notices us, she'll just put it down to our being drunken soldiers, but we can be cunning when we need to be."

Burke was sure they could. Fletcher's men were good.

* * *

William's recovery had been slow but steady and by now he was up and about, though still staying with Batarda's mother. Burke thought he would benefit from the nursing care he was getting there and Juan definitely benefited from the excuse to visit Marta on an almost daily basis.

Now, though, Burke wanted him back on duty. "There's a job you can help me with."

"It's about time too. I'll be getting soft if I get much more of that mothering. And watching young Juan courting is embarrassing. He's besotted, poor lad."

"And Marta?"

"Is a good lass."

This was high praise indeed from William who turned up at Snr Lopez's house the next morning, his uniform brushed and his buttons shined. It was as if he had never been away.

At ten o'clock precisely, Burke took William to stand on Snr Lopez's front steps. Marching down the street came a squad of half a dozen militia men with Juan Batarda leading them. They stopped at the foot of the steps, faced right and snapped a salute towards the house.

William turned to James and stared confused as Burke failed to return the salute.

"Sir?"

"I rather think they are saluting you, Brown."

Burke could have sworn that he saw William blush as he raised his hand to his shako and saluted the militia.

"Fall in now, William. Today's work is officially a Portuguese affair but Major Batarda has kindly agreed that it should be under joint command. Join him at the head of the column, if you please."

One of Lopez's servants stood by, holding Burke's horse.

"I will ride alongside to admire the procession."

They set off in two columns, one headed by Batarda, the other by William. Burke did find them easy to admire. Beresford's efforts to build the Portuguese army into a force that could operate effectively alongside the British was bearing fruit, but Burke suspected that Batarda had been up early in the morning to drill his squad to march as faultlessly as they did now.

As they left the new town and moved towards Alfama, the men struggled to maintain a perfect formation in the narrower streets, but Burke didn't care. It was a pleasure to watch them march so well and he had enjoyed seeing the pride on Batarda's face. Above all, the display was a way of honouring William and all he had suffered.

The drill was impressive, but there was a deadly intent to the morning's exercise. The men were not there just to look pretty. They had a job to do.

Batarda halted his little column outside a house whose cheerful blue door seemed to challenge the dreariness of the street – hardly more than an alley really – that it stood on. Batarda drew his sword and beat on the door with the pommel.

It opened a crack and a woman's face peered out. It was a face that Burke thought must have been beautiful once, but now it was lined with tension and the eyes, peering from under lashes that were still lusciously long, held terror in them.

"Are you known as Beatriz?"

She nodded.

"Come out, please."

For a moment Burke thought she might have slammed the door closed, but then, slowly, she stepped through onto the street. One of the militia men took her gently by the arm and held her while Batarda entered.

Burke handed his horse's reins to another of the militia and followed in.

There was only one floor with a kitchen visible through an open door at the back and one room each side of the entrance. From the room on the right came an angry voice.

"What the hell is going on out there? Beatriz, get your arse in here."

Batarda opened the door and beckoned a puzzled Sgt Brown forward.

Burke saw the moment that William recognised Angelo. Something changed in his face. It was not pretty.

Batarda gestured for two of his men to step forward and take their prisoner, but William raised his and to stop them.

"I'd like a few minutes alone with Mr Angelo, if that would be convenient."

"Are you sure, William?" said Burke. "You're barely recovered."

"I'm sure. You just leave this to me, sir."

"He's probably got a knife. You're unarmed."

"Only fair, sir. Got to give him the chance he never gave me."

Batarda and Burke exchanged glances. Burke nodded and Batarda stepped out of the room, closing the door behind him.

They heard the cry of rage that channelled all the fear and pain that Angelo had inflicted on William and there was the crash of a body being thrown into something wooden that they heard break. After that there was a confusion of noise, a scream, and then silence.

The door opened and Brown stepped out. Burke noticed a cut on his sleeve and some blood staining the fabric. He'd been right about the knife. Otherwise William seemed remarkably undamaged.

"He's alive," he said. "You might want a stretcher for him."

They didn't bother with a stretcher. Two of the militia took a leg each and dragged him into the street, his head striking the cobbles with every step they took.

"We'll deliver him to the castle," said Batarda. "Probably best if you slip away now, William."

William nodded.

James, leading his horse, stepped forward and took William's arm. His sergeant seemed suddenly drained of all emotion and James had to steer him gently back the way they had come.

"Do you feel better now?"

William spoke quietly, like a man waking from a daze. "Better? Yes, sir. It's never quite what you hoped for, is it, sir? But better? Yes, I think I am." And, drawing himself up, he set off at a march, every inch a soldier of the King.

CHAPTER 23: The trap closes

Burke never found out what happened to Angelo. There was suddenly much more to do in army headquarters. Things were moving. It was rumoured that Wellington, after months of inactivity, was heading westward and the French were in pursuit.

Every day, it seemed, Lisbon was filling with more refugees from the north. Some arrived with food harvested from their farms but Wellington, Burke knew, had soldiers combing the countryside north of the Lines, burning everything that could not be carried south. Soon the only food that would be brought into Lisbon would be that carried in by sea.

It was not only food that was being destroyed. Mills were wrecked so that any grain the French discovered could not be ground for bread. Villages were razed to the ground so that the French would have nowhere to shelter. The countryside north of Lisbon was being turned into a desert.

Burke remembered Fletcher explaining this months earlier but it was different now that he was faced with the reality. Lisbon had been crowded before, but now every house was crammed with relatives from outside the city. Both of Snr Lopez's housemaids had sisters in the countryside and William had given up his room to accommodate them, moving to share with James. Yet still the refugees came and the doorways of the new town were filled at night with men and women sheltering there. And, Burke thought, this was barely September. What would happen once winter set in did not bear thinking about.

Angelo's fate could comfortably be left to the Portuguese. Burke was confident that there was nothing he knew about the spy ring that had not already been discovered. Garnier's death had marked the end of the French plot. There was much tidying up to be done, of course. The thugs that the aristocrats had drawn into their exercises in sabotage had to be rounded up and confessions obtained in one way or another. The Portuguese handled that and Burke did not care to learn the details.

Beresford had insisted that the British be responsible for arresting the Portuguese traitors. Burke, he pointed out, was largely responsible for the situation so he could return to his duties as a liaison officer to tidy up the mess. He did smile as he said it, though, and Burke felt that Beresford was perhaps beginning to forgive him for Buenos Aires. He was allowed to keep Batarda to assist him and he took care to make sure that the young man's duties were arranged to allow him as much time as possible with Marta. There had been too much misery and death associated with his time in Lisbon: the least he could do was to help make two people happy.

He sent his report to Colonel Gordon whose reply suggested (without actually saying) that he had done a good job. He suspected that Gordon might be unimpressed with the way that Beresford was clearly angling to take all the credit for the exercise, but Gordon was a realist. In any case, Beresford was as anxious as Gordon to have everything dealt with quietly.

Handling Garnier's underlings and the web of spies and saboteurs he had built up was simple enough. Some went to prison and many ended up "volunteering" to work on the forts that Pereira's enterprise had been trying to spy on. Burke appreciated the irony. A few of the men who knew too much, or who had just annoyed their Portuguese captors, quietly vanished. Lisbon, like all ports, had its share of robberies in the narrow alleys and these sometimes ended fatally. A few more missing men attracted no attention.

The aristocratic traitors were more of a problem. They were not the sort of people who could quietly vanish without anybody noticing and Beresford was anxious not to hold trials that would expose rifts between the British Army and elements of Portuguese society. It was Burke's job to talk to them, sorting the venal from the young and foolish. Not all of them had realised the scale of the French operation. They felt all they were doing was offering aid to their friends who were fighting alongside the French. Yes, they knew that it was technically treason but they did not feel like traitors. There were whole regiments that had gone over to Napoleon and nobody was suggesting that they all be hanged.

Talking to them, Burke felt very old. They were, in their own peculiar way, idealistic. They had thought that helping Napoleon unite

Europe in a new, modern world was a noble aim. Now, faced with the reality of the deaths that their games had led to and the prospect of their own lives ending in the hangman's noose, they were having to radically review their life choices.

Burke's reports often concluded that there was no real danger that these young men would damage their country again. They could be released with a warning and the knowledge that they would be watched for the rest of their lives. Their post would be opened, their servants would be paid to spy on them and they might well be encouraged never to leave Lisbon. It was hardly escaping scot-free, but it was vastly preferable to the alternative.

To his relief, Beresford was generally happy to agree with his recommendations. Not all the traitors, though, were young and idealistic. Sometimes extreme measures were called for. Even then, though, a public trial and execution was to be avoided.

Morais was killed in a hunting accident. Burke was pleased to hear it though he was a little surprised, as he had never heard of Morais hunting. Perhaps it was his inexperience that led to the accident that killed him. Carvalho had been to his hunting lodge to assess the damage from the fire and had been struck by falling masonry. William had wanted to be the man with the masonry but Burke vetoed that idea. It was best to stay well away and keep their hands clean.

Burke spent long days at his desk, interrogating his aristocratic prisoners, reassuring the locals that all was well with the alliance, and writing page after page of reports which were all sent to Beresford and which, he suspected, were filed away somewhere without ever being read.

So September slipped away in a welter of paperwork. Out there in the real world, though, the armies were moving with Wellington drawing nearer and nearer to Torres Vedras and the French, under Masséna, following.

Fletcher kept Burke informed. There was no official reason why he needed to know where Wellington was, but, even now, they were not many people that Fletcher felt that he could confide in and he enjoyed telling Burke how Wellington's plans were progressing. William, too, kept Burke up to date with the latest news. How he obtained his information, which was frequently better than that circulated to staff officers, baffled Burke. In all his years with William, though, he had learned that the gossip of NCOs in the British Army spreads news faster than any network of couriers that generals might set up.

On 10 October 1810 the British Army passed behind the Lines of Torres Vedras and Wellington's trap was sprung. When Masséna arrived at the Lines the French could advance no further but, with nothing to forage behind them, a retreat would be a disaster. Fletcher's great defensive work meant that they were trapped in the desert the Portuguese had created, devoid of food or fuel as winter set in.

Although Wellington's troops were not based in the town, Portuguese and British soldiers found every reason, legitimate or otherwise, to spend time in Lisbon, adding to the chaos caused by the civilian refuges and the sailors who came and went with the convoys bringing food supplies. Troops patrolled the streets to keep order and Beresford and his liaison officers were busy from dawn to dusk, settling arguments about billeting, arranging food distribution, reassuring prominent citizens that provision would be made for relatives travelling in from their estates north of the lines, and dealing with complaints about profiteering. Even Snr Lopez was pulled in to help: after his work on Pereira's accounts he could spot inflated prices in just a few minutes spent with a grocer's books.

Burke would return to Lopez's home which he now shared with a cousin from Caldas da Rainha, north of the Lines, as well as the maids' sisters and, he suspected, a family living unofficially in the stable block behind it. His work left him tired but content. It might not be glamorous or involve leading troops into battle, but it was the sort of staff-work that any general relies on in warfare. Dealing with captured traitors was something he was happy to leave to Beresford.

Beresford, on the other hand, was happy to leave them to Burke.

The men Burke had identified as merely misguided and foolish had long since been released. The likes of Morais and Carvalho were dead. That left only those who could not be trusted at liberty in Lisbon yet who hardly merited execution. They were left in limbo, languishing in gaol, albeit in relatively comfortable circumstances (they were aristocrats after all) until November, with nobody taking any responsibility for what was to happen to them. It wasn't until almost the end of the month that Beresford asked, after another meeting about food distribution, when the last of the prisoners had been released.

"I have no idea, sir. I've reported on their interrogation and left the papers with you."

"You did? And what did you recommend?"

"They're no threat to us now. The French know all about the Lines and with the forts all manned nobody is going to be passing messages across to Masséna's men."

"How many are there left?"

"Just four, sir."

The clerk came in with papers to be signed and Burke waited while Beresford worked his way through them. By the time the last one had been carefully blotted off with sand and the clerk had taken them away, Beresford had reached a decision.

"I'm not having them back in society spreading their poison, but it would not help to hang them. Just four, eh? Looks like an insignificant plot by a few malcontents. Let's give them a Christmas present. We'll let them go, take them up to the Lines, give them horses and turn a blind eye while they run back to the French. I'll make sure there's a paragraph gazetting it and everyone who matters will see a few pathetic scoundrels running away from justice. That should do the trick. See to it, can you, Burke?"

And Burke saw to it.

William, on hearing the news, suggested they celebrate with a drink. "We should be home soon."

"I'm not sure what Gordon has in mind, but I'm hoping he'll leave us here long enough to attend Batarda's wedding. It seems Marta is to make an honest man of him."

"There's a lot to be said for marriage," said William.

Burke thought of Molly in her tavern near the Tower. William might hardly ever be there, but it was home: a place to return to when the fighting was done. And now Batarda would have a home, with Marta to welcome him back after battle. And him? He had his quarters in the Tower until Gordon summoned him for his next mission.

"We can have a drink to celebrate," said William.

Burke thought of the spies who had been hanged and the ones who were disgraced and the men who had fled to the north. He thought of

Sra Pereira and her son, mourning the traitor's death. And he thought of Garnier and their last drink together.

'A drink to celebrate.' He had been at war all his adult life and there was no sign of an end to it, but there were still good things to drink to.

"Yes," he said to William. "Let's have a drink. Better yet, let's have a lot of drinks." He had, after all, plenty to celebrate. He was alive. William was alive. In a country ravaged by war and in a city full of hungry people he would eat well that night and sleep in a feather bed, even if he would share the room with William, who snored prodigiously.

Tonight he would forget about the spies and the dead. Napoleon and his armies and his plots would wait.

Tonight he was going to get very, very drunk. He could worry about the war tomorrow.

THE END

HISTORICAL NOTE

Ever since I heard of the Lines of Torres Vedras, I've wanted to see them and in 2019 I finally did. Even after over 200 years a lot of the forts that made up this astonishing defensive line are still there. (You can see the remains of one of the smaller forts at the bottom right of the cover.) I decided I had to write a book about them.

We visited Lisbon too and I thought that would be a lovely venue for an evil plot.

The trouble with a novel about the Lines of Torres Vedras is that very little happened at the lines. With the exception of a single probing attack by Masséna, there was no military action there at all. The interlinking string of forts was so strong that Masséna simply didn't bother to try to break them.

That doesn't mean that the Lines were a waste of resources. On the contrary, Wellington's plan worked well. Masséna's army lost thousands of men from starvation, and hundreds of deserters surrendered to Wellington.

The French managed to find stores of food that (against Wellington's orders) Portuguese peasants had hidden in the hope of recovering them later. Without these supplies, French casualties might have been much greater. The Portuguese and British military did not suffer from hunger but Portuguese civilians died in very large numbers. Even after the French had abandoned Portugal, the civilian population suffered from the loss of their olive trees, which had been cut down ahead of the French advance.

When the French were finally forced to retreat from the Lines, the French continued to take casualties as they were harried by Wellington's army. Masséna's total casualties may have been up to 25,000 men as well as massive losses of cannons and other equipment.

The battles with the retreating French are a gift to writers of military history (Bernard Cornwell stands out here) but not much use to people like me who are writing stories of espionage.

Fortunately we know that there was an active spy ring in Lisbon and that four spies fled north to the French at the very end of December 1810. The story of *Burke and the Lines of Torres Vedras* is built around that nugget of historical fact. The rest, though, is entirely my imagination.

Colonel Fletcher was a real person as was General Beresford. Beresford and the real James Burke may well have met during the invasion of Buenos Aires, in which they were both involved (see *Burke and the Land of Silver*). My depiction of Beresford could be unfair but I took against him because of his mishandling of events in Argentina and I admit to allowing my prejudice full rein here. Beresford did definitely do an excellent job in reorganising the Portuguese army, and I have tried to give him credit for this.

As ever, odd bits of real history keep breaking through into the story. William's tale about the colonel being asked for leave is mentioned in John Le Couteur's account of his service in the War of 1812 in North America. (*Merry Hearts Make Light Days* edited by D E Graves and published by Carleton University Press in Ottawa.)

Wellington was indeed an enthusiastic huntsman and there is an account of his fox hunting on his campaigns in Mary Evans' article *Hound, Horn And View Halloo For Waterloo* in Sports Illustrated, 3 Feb 1969.

'Softly, softly catchee monkey' was not a common phrase in those days but had entered into English usage around the turn of the century. It is thought to have originated in West Africa and may have been more common amongst troops, having been brought back by those who had served there.

The 'pease' that came up with the supplies is not a misprint. Pease (as in pease pudding) was essentially mushy peas boiled up into a sort of pudding. You can buy tins of it in many supermarkets today, if you want to try it. (I recommend pickle with it, or something else that will add flavour.)

Garnier's snuffbox (the one he kept his hemlock in) is based on an actual box that was recently sold in Australia.

Thank you

Thanks first to my wife, Tammy. This is traditional, I know, but in her case especially well-deserved. She is not only generally supportive of my writing but she listens to me reading key sections aloud. She is the first to see my draft copies and she is happy to praise the bits she thinks work and to savage the bits that don't. She also proofreads with the dedication of someone who was diagnosed dyslexic as a child and has fought through by checking and re-checking her own work and, now, my efforts.

My son gets pulled in for comments before anyone but Tammy has seen it and then come beta readers. Readers for this one included Paul Benedyk (who would make a wonderful professional proof-reader), John Haines and Stacy Townend.

The errors that remain and the bits you don't like are, of course, entirely down to me.

Cover design is by Dave Slaney. Dave does all my books and is very, very good at it.

My thanks go to everyone who helped and to you, dear reader, for supporting me with your attention. And special thanks to those of you who go online to Amazon or Goodreads and leave a review. Reviews are not just gratifying to authors (we do like to think people have enjoyed what we write) but also invaluable in generating sales. We're not looking for literary essays – just a sentence or two will help.

Burke will be back ...

I hope you have enjoyed *Burke and the Lines of Torres Vedras*. This is the seventh book about James Burke. Do take a look at the others if you haven't already. They haven't been written in chronological order so you can read them in whatever order you want, but the first is *Burke in the Land of Silver* which is the one most closely based on the real James Burke's life (yes, he really existed) so it's an obvious place to start.

If you want to learn more about the books and the world that James Burke lived in, I recommend that you have a look at my website: http://tomwilliamsauthor.co.uk where you can sign up to my newsletter and be the first to hear about new books. You can also follow me on Facebook (https://www.facebook.com/AuthorTomWilliams) and Twitter (https://twitter.com/TomCW99).

I'm sure you've seen notes from authors before asking that you review their books on Amazon, but it really makes a huge difference. Without a big marketing budget (and hardly any authors are given those), Amazon reviews are crucial to getting books to an audience. If you have enjoyed *Burke and the Lines of Torres Vedras* and would like other people to have a chance to enjoy it too, it would be so helpful if you could write a few words on Amazon. Just a sentence or two saying that you liked it and you think others might is all it takes – we're not talking about the Times Literary Supplement here. I do read all my reviews (writers who say they don't are almost certainly fibbing) and I love getting them.

Thank you again for reading.

OTHER BOOKS BY TOM WILLIAMS

James Burke, spy

Burke in the Land of Silver

Burke and the Bedouin

Burke at Waterloo

Burke in the Peninsula

Burke in Ireland

Burke and the Pimpernel Affair

The Williamson Papers

The White Rajah

Cawnpore

Back Home

Contemporary Urban Fantasy

Dark Magic

Something Wicked

Eat the Poor

Printed in Great Britain
by Amazon

21291605R00112